Also By Joe Moore

Return of the Birds

The Santa Claus Trilogy

Believe Again, The North Pole Chronicles
1st Book in the Trilogy
Faith, Hope & Reindeer
2nd Book in the Trilogy
Glaciers Melt & Mountains Smoke
3rd Book in the Trilogy

Santa's Elf Series©

Santa's World, Introducing Santa's Elf Series
Jamie Hardrock, Chief Mining Elf
Shelley Wrapitup, Master Design Elf
Keeney Eagleye, Naughty/Nice List Manager
Sarah Buttons, Master Doll Maker
Ford MacHarley, Master Wheelsmith
Carol Joynote, Chief Music Coordinator

The Faces of Krampus

The Christmas Eve Journey

Santa's Famous Incredible, Flying Reindeer

The Santa Claus Enigma

REVENGE OF THE BIRDS

by

Joe Moore

Published by
The North Pole Press

Published by The North Pole Press

Smoky Mountains, Tennessee

ISBN13: 978-1-7324958-9-0

Cover design by Mary Moore

Library of Congress Control Number 2019905946

Information about and for this book may be obtained through contacting North Pole
Press at: Info@thenorthpolepress.com.
Printed in the United States of America

Dedication

We all have people that inspire us and cause us to be better people than we currently are. My dear friend Lynnda Manville, is the person who inspires me to always reach out to be more extraordinary than I thought I could be. This book is dedicated to her as a thank you for making me a better person and citizen by thinking more of others.

Acknowledgments

There are always so many more people behind the scenes of every book. Whether they are ever acknowledged or not, they are a blessing to any author. Of course there are the easy and obvious ones. For me they always include my greatest fan and supporter, my lovely wife, Mary. No matter what project I am working on, she is always encouraging me and looking over my shoulder (when I ask) offering suggestions and inspiration for my stories.

The editor for my last three works has also become invaluable to me. Gary Brown has probably forgotten more about writing than I ever hope to learn. His suggestions far exceed my best efforts in trying to convey my stories. His many decades of journalism experience and expertise that he has applied to these books has made whatever I write extraordinarily better for my readers. Thanks Gary for being such an integral part of everything I do.

Another "behind the scenes" partner I have is Jane Tiller, our representative at Ingram/Lightning Source. I cannot thank her enough for all the help and support she has shown me personally, and the North Pole Press in general. Jane has assisted us in every part of the publishing process, including working with us on new programs and opportunities in the massive Ingram publishing/distribution world. She is a great asset and a good friend.

Other authors, librarians, friends, and most importantly – my readers, make up the bulk of the people I am grateful to acknowledge. There are too many to list, and that is becoming a wonderful problem to have. Please know I am eternally grateful to each and every one of you. That said, I need to to say a special thank you to Lin and J.L. Stepp, Susan Dorsey, and my very special fans, Henry Greenwood (who became a central character in this book) and Alex Wilson. These people have shown me an incredible amount of support and assistance during my writing exploits. You are all very dear to me.

I hope people enjoy this as much they did "Return", and as much as I enjoyed writing this.

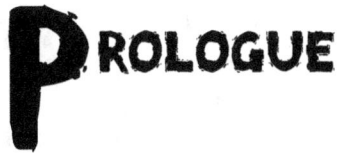ROLOGUE

Before the events of San Clemente, California, no one would have believed that birds could become rabid. But the death of a sole Cockatoo disproved everything they previously believed. Now the authorities thought they had stopped the pandemic from spreading. The birds that were infected by the newly discovered Super Aviary Rabies Virus had thankfully been eliminated by the military and local law enforcement, or died off naturally from the disease.

People that had been attacked were still receiving rabies vaccinations to stem the deadly effects of the disease, but their chances of survival were now good. A relative few had thought their brush with the birds was so minor that they did not need to seek medical attention. It was a fatal mistake. Even the most minor scratch later infected the patient to a point where the vaccine could not contain the virus from spreading, and they lost the battle for their life. Other than these unfortunate souls, most people had been spared the painful infection and death, thanks to the SARV rabies vaccine, which was still being flown in daily to treat the hundreds of patients needing the injection.

It had only been a matter of days since the rabid birds had attacked and killed hundreds and injured many hundreds more at the San Clemente Pier. People were trying to put their lives back together and constantly kept an eye to the sky above in case any rabid birds remained. There were very few birds at all, and most of these were small songbirds and not infected. Warnings from the CDC continued to flood the airwaves advising people to be vigilant of gathering birds, and to seek immediate medical attention if they had any altercation with a bird, wild or domestic.

The gulls that stopped in San Clemente, California, had eaten their fill and were on the move again. They had made it up the coast to Laguna Beach after beginning their migration from Mexico several days before. They had a long way to go to Mono Lake but had been doing well. They were making progress covering the vast expanse that lay before them.

But now they had trouble focusing their intention to make it to their nesting grounds. Something was growing in their minds with ever-increasing urgency. Got to eat, gotta eat, GOTTA EAT! It had dominated their thoughts soon after they filled their bellies in San Clemente. First beginning as a whisper, it now screamed in their heads continuously, often blocking out their inherent need to reach their nesting ground to mate and continue their species.

While there were loads of people walking the streets and beaches in Laguna, the flock hadn't found anything to eat until they made it to Emerald Bay. There they saw a giant ball of fish boiling at the surface and immediately dove into the frenzy before them. They were not alone, and many of the resident gulls and other seabirds like California Brown Pelicans and the endangered California Least Tern were fishing with them.

As the gulls snapped up the fish, some either escaped their beaks at the last moment or were cut in half at the speed of the attack. Those pieces were grabbed by the other birds and immediately ingested.

And that's how it all began, again.

CHAPTER ONE

It had only been a few days since the injection of the antivirus to bird attack victims and the death of the remaining infected birds. Many things were slowly returning to normal. Professor Ellen Revere had flown back to Cornell and was working at her lab on further applications of the Super Aviary Rabies Virus. Tory McKnight and Dr. Bill Forrester were at the University of California at San Diego working on the vaccine that would cure all the species of infected birds, and prevent further outbreaks.

The dreaded Super Aviary Rabies Virus that caused the bird disease in San Clemente could still become a serious problem. They had a variety of strains they thought might possibly work, but could not be sure until they field-tested each one on infected birds.

While the two were hunched over their own microscopes, Dr. Forrester's wife, Natalie, walked in carrying sacks from a local fast-food restaurant.

Tory looked up at her and said smiling, "So that is why my stomach is making all that noise."

"Is it really noon already?" asked Dr. Forrester.

Natalie came up and giving him a quick peck on the cheek said. "Try 1:30, my dear. I knew you would be starving this poor girl, so I took the liberty of getting you both something to eat."

Tory thanked Natalie and immediately dove into the

contents of the bag.

"So? Any progress? I thought you would be out and about preventing any possibility of a recurrence of the San Clemente incident by now," said Natalie.

Dr. Forrester rubbed the two-day growth on his face and said, "We would if we weren't missing a critical element in all this."

Tory snickered and said, "Yeah, test subjects."

Natalie asked, "Has no one found the possibility of an infected bird anywhere around San Clemente?"

"Only a few birds are living in San Clemente at all, and none of them show signs of the infection. And trying to catch a healthy bird is quite a challenge at any time. Plus we can't be sure a canary or parakeet would exhibit the same elements of the disease those birds did," Dr. Forrester said poking at the dead gull in front of him.

"Besides," continued Tory, "While we can infect a healthy bird, it would be better to get one already infected to guarantee we are treating the original infection versus one introduced in the lab."

A formal triumvirate had been established among the Center for Disease Control, the Orange County Sheriff's Department, and the University of California-San Diego to watch for any suspected activity of abnormal bird behavior, especially bird attacks or large flocking throughout the Orange County area.

This watch stretched from as far south as Oceanside all the way up to Long Beach. Since nothing had taken place in the other counties, the various agencies thought anything peculiar would appear in this area first. Since the "die-off," as they called it, nothing unusual had taken place.

Natalie shook her head, "I can't believe every single bird infected dropped dead. I mean, I have to say I'm glad they did. This disease could have spread like wildfire. But still, it just amazes me nothing was left."

"Except all the bodies," sighed Tory, "They are still losing people over at the Medical Center. Chris told me two more people passed away yesterday."

Chris Palmer was Tory's boyfriend and was responsible for discovering the epidemic in San Clemente. He was a full-time lifeguard when the incidents began and had witnessed the first attacks on people. He was now working at Saddleback Memorial as a medical intern and studying for his medical degree.

Dr. Forrester said, "We knew this was going to happen. Too many people received the treatment too late to stop the disease. Thank God we got to as many with the vaccine as we did, or we could have lost far more."

"Yeah, like me," said Natalie. Natalie Forrester was one of the survivors from a bird attack at the San Clemente Pier. She had received a nasty scratch while fleeing with her husband, Tory, and Chris from the fatal onslaught while at a festival.

"It still spooks me to think if we hadn't come up with the virus in time..." and Dr. Forrester's voice trailed off.

Natalie got up and gave him a smile, saying, "Ah, but you did, and I am here to prove it."

Dr. Forrester smiled back at his wife and patted the hand that had the injury from the bird.

"At least you are not having to treat more new

patients," added Natalie.

"Yes, but that doesn't bring us any closer to solving this problem," said Tory.

"And this is just the same as that time in Bodega Bay before this?" asked Natalie.

"Apparently," answered Dr. Forrester while chewing on some French fries. "The birds just suddenly died off as if their bodies instantly shut down, all at the same time. According to what we can piece together, it took longer this time. which could mean the virus was stronger or its effects weaker, we just don't know."

"And without a living specimen, we can't see if this vaccine would completely eradicate the virus, put it into remission, or just weaken its effects," said Tory.

"Assuming it had any effect at all," said Dr. Forrester. "We won't know if it works fast enough to combat the disease. We are dealing with a very high metabolism in birds. Every day that gets by us lessens the chance we can find a bird in time to counteract the infection."

They had plenty of dead infected birds and multiple vials of their fluids handy, but the disease changed once the body died, and they could not be sure they were working with the same properties as a living host might have. The CDC confirmed their suspicions and said that they, too, thought the disease was not necessarily the same after death, even though it would still be highly contagious to any animal that came into contact with a carcass.

Natalie felt the frustration of the two scientists. So trying to lighten things, she asked Tory, "So how is Chris doing at the Medical Center?

Chris Palmer had accepted Dr. Forrester's offer to enter the medical program at UCSD, and his first project was to assist the remaining patients in San Clemente. He was also still filling in part-time as a lifeguard when needed.

Tory shrugged, "Being back at Saddleback Memorial, we talk daily, but he is into his studies and working with patients, and I am into this. We don't have as much to say to each other right now. We are hoping to get together next weekend if he can get the time off between his guard duties and the hospital."

Deciding that was the wrong subject as well, Natalie asked her husband, "Have you heard from Ellen?"

Dr. Forrester looked up smiling and said, "I'll thank you not to mention that woman's name in front of me. She is taking the best assistant I'll ever have away from me in less than a month. I will be forced to go back and do all my own work until I can find a decent assistant again. And of course, they will be distantly inferior to Miss McKnight."

Tory smiled at his comment. She was anxious to be working with one of the leading people in her chosen field of Ornithology, but would also regret leaving Dr. Forrester and San Diego for Cornell University. *Everything is a trade-off,* she thought to herself.

Professor Ellen Revere was also working on a vaccine for the birds, but she decided to try the virus on mammals to make sure that the antivirus had the same positive results as it did on the humans they had treated. Because there were no known infected mammals on the loose, she had decided to infect her test subjects. There was no other way to make sure the disease wouldn't spread through the animal kingdom.

"So far, she is still hopeful for positive conclusions with her experiments," said Dr. Forrester. "We believe that the virus doesn't mutate in mammals as we might have first feared. Of course, she has the same problem having to infect the animals artificially. Again, we can only hope the cure would work in the wild."

"Well that's still good news," Natalie beamed.

Dr. Forrester and Tory just nodded alternately munching on their lunch and looking back into their microscopes. Natalie, decided it was time to leave them to their work having completed her mission to feed them. She asked her husband if he would be home in time for dinner and extended an invitation to Tory.

Dr. Forrester said, "I should be, yes."

Tory excused herself from the invite saying she had several personal projects including laundry needing to be done, but requested a rain check.

"Anytime," Natalie said as she opened the door and said goodbye to them. Once through the door, she began scratching the area on her hand where she received the injury from the bird in San Clemente. "Damn thing, never stops itching" she mumbled to herself as she walked down the hall.

ᚲᚲᚲᚲ ᚲᚲᚲᚲ ᚲᚲᚲᚲ ᚲᚲᚲ ᚲᚲᚲᚲ ᚲᚲᚲᚲ ᚲᚲᚲᚲ

The gulls had filled their bellies with enough fish for the moment. Usually, it would have been enough to suppress their cravings, but some of the gulls still felt

the urge to continue feeding. Most of the other birds had
already flown off, with the pelicans being the first to
leave. The California Gulls from San Clemente were still
snapping at the remaining birds and any floating pieces
of fish.

Eventually, the resident birds returned to the shore,
and only the migrating birds were left floating in the
surf. These birds seemed to fight the instinct between
continuing their migration north and searching for more
food.

The migrating gulls were far more aggressive in their
feeding frenzy than the local birds, a few of which
became injured when they got too close. None had been
seriously hurt, but a few had nasty cuts that would take
time to heal.

The migrating gulls finally flew off. They followed a
different pattern from previous years, as they flew
further inland than before. They were searching for food
caches that they could grab as they continued their
journey. Even though they had just fed, their minds were
forever focused on their next meal. Gotta eat.

ᴋ ᴋ ᴋ ᴋ ᴋ ᴋ ᴋ ᴋ ᴋ ᴋ ᴋ ᴋ ᴋ ᴋ ᴋ ᴋ ᴋ ᴋ ᴋ ᴋ

Dr. Alice Friedman, the Deputy Director for
Preparedness and Emerging Infections at the Center for
Disease Control, was packing up her office at Saddleback
Memorial Health Center. This had been ground zero
during the bird attacks and had housed dozens of CDC
employees and medical personnel from all over Orange
County, California.

The facility had been pushed to its maximum during the previous weeks. It finally was returning to its usual activities. Now the rabies victims only occupied one small wing of the center and a handful of beds. These patients were made as comfortable as possible, but their prognosis was not good.

Dr. Friedman had sent almost all the CDC employees from Atlanta back home and was at long last happy to be returning, herself. Southern California was beautiful, but this had hardly been a vacation. She was anxious to get home to her own home and family.

Almost immediately after the die-off of the birds, she let Dr. Grant Abernathy, who headed up Animal Resources – Biologics branch, fly back to Atlanta with the stipulation that he would be on the first plane back if anything about this case resurfaced.

Dr. Anna Lanz with the CDC was the first to hear about this disease. She would be staying a while longer and monitoring the remaining patients. She was enjoying her stay in Southern California since the epidemic had died out with the birds, and was single, anyway.

She entered Dr. Friedman's office and asked, "All packed?"

Dr. Friedman looked up, "Almost. As usual, I have more paperwork than luggage to bring back with me. I even planned a long stay with lots of clothes," she said shaking her head.

"Our agency loves nothing more than their paper," laughed Dr. Lanz. "Even with all the computer files and ease of access to that, they still demand their paper trail."

Dr. Friedman looked at the stack of boxes and shrugged, "I guess they are worried we may have an EMP meltdown, or worse."

She then looked squarely at Dr. Lanz, "Now, you will keep me posted if the least little thing happens, right? I don't care how insignificant you think it may be. We were lucky this time. I can't believe how close we all came to a major national pandemic. If those birds hadn't died off and instead flown to other areas..."

Dr. Lanz said, "You have my promise. Nothing will take place without you immediately hearing it from me."

Dr. Friedman shook Dr. Lanz's hand and then signaled for the others waiting to take all her possessions to the car heading to the airport.

Even before the attack on the San Clemente Pier, something happened that no one would have considered. The first vulture that had contracted the SARV disease had succumbed to its effects, and like the others that would follow, had fallen dead.

It happened in a field outside of town and was not witnessed. Because of the other vultures that took part in the attacks, no one would have thought that one of their numbers was missing. There were just too many birds involved to consider that one or two might have died earlier.

At first, the corpse wasn't noticed. But, as the smell of decay began to increase, others picked up the scent.

The first was two turkey vultures in the vicinity that had not been previously infected. They picked at the corpse first. Soon after a coyote ventured by, followed by a couple raccoons, all of which made short work of the body.

It wasn't long before the remains had disappeared completely. The animals and birds carried something of the vulture away with them. Something none of them would have wanted.

Within a few days, the coyote had limited its foraging only to the night. The sun was too bright and hurt its eyes and head too much to hunt during the day. While it was always hungry and thirsty, the idea of drinking water was loathing to him because his throat hurt so badly.

Food was all the coyote craved. It was always particularly adept at hunting, but now it was continuously foraging for anything that moved or was already dead. Its belly was extended from all the meals it had consumed. Killing the animals now gave it as much pleasure as eating them.

The coyote hated anything and everything.

The same happened with the raccoons. They already did the majority of their foraging at night. But now they were always ready to eat anything they came across, day or night. They already knew where they could find a steady source of food, as they had robbed from people in the past. So they made their way to the trash cans of the nearby residents, and with each passing day, they became bolder and less frightened of the neighborhood dogs, cats, and people.

In fact, they hoped something would get in their path so they could attack it, kill it, and eat it.

Although there were very few vultures in the area now, the two newly infected vultures began to extend their range much farther than ever before. They were combing far and wide to locate any remains that might help satisfy their appetite. They had not joined up with the other birds who were wreaking havoc in San Clemente as they acquired their unending appetite after the die-off.

As they continued their foraging, they left their roosting areas and headed to new regions around the Southland and extended their circle further north. Riding the thermals, they headed toward Dana Point.

ᴋ ᴋᵗᴋ ᴋ ᴋᵗᴋ ᴋ ᴋᵗᴋ ᴋ ᴋᵗ ᴋ ᴋᵗᴋ ᴋ ᴋᵗᴋ ᴋ ᴋᵗᴋ

At the top of the twenty-story Park Place Tower in Irvine, a successful mother was raising her fourth set of chicks. Over the last few years, she had fledged five out of seven nestlings and was about to add two more to her count. Her efforts, along with that of her mate, added several thriving Peregrine Falcons to the population of Southern California.

While the birds before her were within mere days of taking wing, she and her mate were still providing all the food they had to have. This was the toughest year so far for keeping her brood fed. In previous years, there were many more pigeons and rodents to catch. This year it seemed most of the pigeons had moved elsewhere, and many of the rodents had been killed off from the overzealous owners of the high rises.

She was having to travel further out to catch the next meal for the family. This left the chicks vulnerable for more extended periods, but there was little choice. It was this or have them starve. Luckily for the mating pair, they were almost at the end of this season's parenthood.

As she heard her the cries of her mate coming, she knew it was her turn to venture off for the next meal. She hopped up on the railing, unfurled her wings, and took off to feed her family.

The migrating gulls had been following Highway 1 along the coast for most of the time. Now they were moving deeper inland and headed toward more traffic and increased populations. Most of what they saw was neighborhood dogs and a few animals that were too fast for them to catch. Once away from the water, they needed to scavenge more than hunt for fish.

The gulls had now come up to the I-5 freeway and were deep into the residential areas. They were still scouring the area looking for roadkill or a garbage dump. They knew by instinct and from their previous forays that landfills and dump sites were virtual buffets of food. Their insatiable appetites drove them on.

Most of the time these treasure troves were loaded with other birds. This was never a problem as there was plenty to go around, and it also made the landfills easy to spot from the air. They were focused on the ground below them when it happened.

One of the gulls that had opened its wings to glide for a bit, suddenly felt the searing pain of the talons cut through its back and right side. It let out a terrible shriek, but it was too late. The falcon was already maneuvering its catch back toward the nest. The other gulls picked up the pace of their flight in case the bird's mate or other threat was lurking nearby.

While the peregrine hardly looked big enough to attack the larger bird, its strength and experience more than compensated for the size of its prey. The gull was dead by the time the falcon reached the tower, the talons and an occasional beak thrust having done its work.

This was a feast for the family, and soon all four birds were throwing feathers in every direction. The mother had once again assured the survival of her two new chicks and the propagation of her species.

CHAPTER TWO

Professor Ellen Revere was studying the effects of SARV on six mice she had infected from the birds Cornell had on hand. She had been studying them for a couple days and was amazed at the results the disease had on them.

She had the mice in three different cages, with a pair in each. She had the pens close to each other and found that the mice kept trying to get together. Most of the time at least four of the mice huddled together with the other two pushing against the cage as close as they could get to the other mice.

This was interesting to her considering the increased agitation and aggressiveness of the mice. They were snapping at anything that seemed to annoy them. They also stopped drinking water altogether. In fact, they would not go anywhere near the bottles that hung on the side of the cages.

They were off their food, too. Even though the bowls were filled with the usual food given their lab specimens. Prof. Revere thought by now they had to be starving.

Prof. Revere had been thinking of the ferocity of the San Clemente birds and purposely brought some fresh hamburger from home that day. She placed the meat next to the cage. Instantly, all six mice began scampering around trying to get to the meat.

She donned her gloves and took a chunk and placed it

in the center cage. Both mice had charged the meat and devoured it at a speed that would have been hard to imagine if she had not seen it herself. Further, the other mice were trying to get as close as they could and were squealing with frustration and anger.

She took some more of the meat and placed it into a second cage at the opposite end. She barely got her fingers out as the mice ravenously attacked the hamburger. Having finished the meat in their cage, the center pair of mice were now at that same end, as well, screeching and scratching at the other cage.

Prof. Revere thought the amount of meat she provided would have sufficed for the first pair. But they were acting like the pair that received none to this point.

She gave them the same amount again, confident that their little bodies couldn't eat much more. She was stunned as she watched them consume every bit. Moreover, the mice who had nothing up to this point were now continually screeching and racing all over their cage in a constant fury.

She repeated the experiment giving the third set of mice some hamburger. This time one of the mice had bit the glove but missed her finger. It attacked the meat with a ferocity she had never witnessed in mice before.

Prof. Revere knew what she needed to do next, but was uncomfortable about the prospect. She went into another part of the lab and extracted another mouse from a cage. This mouse had not been infected with the virus, and she was sure she was sending it to its immediate death.

She barely opened the center cage enough to squeeze

the new mouse in. She watched as the two mice who had finished with their food back the new mouse into a corner. She was videotaping the whole experiment and wondered if she had the stamina to watch this firsthand. She was surprised at what she witnessed next.

One of the mice approached closer and then regurgitated part of its meal before the new mouse. Prof. Revere had not heard of such behavior in normal mammalian rabies, nor did it seem possible mice would have this amount of thought process. It was tough to believe what she just witnessed. The mouse approached the food and began eating. Satisfied, the other two mice moved back toward where the food was dispensed licking the bars for more.

She continued to watch as the mice continued to snap at the air around them but showed no aggression to the other mouse or each other. She wished she could go into the cage and retrieve the third mouse, but knew the moment the professor stuck her hand in there, she would be attacked by the other two mice.

Her lab assistant came through the door, and Prof. Revere played the video for him. Upon completion, she asked him to go to the store and get some fresh meat that wasn't ground. She now knew what her next experiments would be for the seven mice.

ᴋ ᴋᵗᴋ ᴋ ᴋᵗᴋ ᴋ ᴋᵗᴋ ᴋ ᴋᵗ ᴋ ᴋᵗᴋ ᴋ ᴋᵗᴋ ᴋ ᴋᵗᴋ

The raccoons were on the move. They were racing from one trash can to another, pushing over the cans and digging through the contents. They had to investigate every can because they were looking for particular substances. While raccoons were omnivorous, these specific animals were now anything but. They had to have meat. The fresher, the better.

They passed up pizza unless it had meat on it, they ignored the canned food contents, and even discarded cooked food with or without meat in it. Instead, they chewed on bones, especially raw ones and other uncooked treats they found.

They made a terrible mess and were moving from one house to the next, their appetites insatiable. In one yard they were tearing through the trash when they heard barking behind them. They slowly pulled their heads out of the large green trash can to see a boxer growling at them.

They bared their teeth at the large dog, but he didn't budge and just growled back. The raccoons moved slowly to either side of the dog. At first, the dog was confused as to which raccoon to focus on. He then saw one had moved closer to him than the other and made his decision.

He jumped at the nearer of the two raccoons and tried to bite the animal on its neck. The raccoon moved much faster than the dog thought it could and attacked the dogs flank instead of being in front of him. The second raccoon was on his other back leg and bit its tail and backside.

The boxer yelped and somehow fought its way loose of the two raccoons. It ran off and through a dog door into its house. When the owner of the dog came into the kitchen where the dog laid, she screamed looking at the blood running off the dog's haunches. She called her veterinarian and made an emergency appointment for the boxer. She was told to bring the dog in quickly.

The raccoons found as much as they cared for in that trash can, and realized they had missed the meal that had just been presented to them, so they moved on to the next house. They adeptly crawled up the six-foot wall and over into the next yard.

Dr. Joanne Miller was examining the wound to the protestations of the boxer. "It's okay Buster, I know it hurts, but I have to see how bad it got you."

Dr. Miller wasn't sure if it was only one animal as there were lacerations on both sides, which might have indicated either one large animal or a couple. The main concern was the nasty bite Buster had received on his one flank and tail.

"I'm afraid this is going to need some stitches and an overnight stay for Buster," Dr. Miller said to Buster's owner. "I already checked his chart, and he is up to date on all his shots. In fact, Buster just got his rabies booster just six months ago, so we do not have to be concerned about that."

The owner nodded her head and said, "I always do what you and your office recommends. We plan to have Buster around a good long while."

"I don't suppose you saw what attacked him?" asked the veterinarian.

"No, I heard some commotion out in the back yard and was about to check it out when I heard Buster yelping and come through our doggy door," replied the owner.

"Well, Mrs. Hastings, I suggest you carefully look around your yard. I would say this is a large enough bite that it could be a possum, raccoon or another larger animal. Not a cat, but maybe a bobcat," Dr. Miller shook her head saying, "I can't be sure, but you should be careful when you look around."

Mrs. Hasting said, "We have had some real problems recently with raccoons getting into our trash. They have become a real nuisance through the whole neighborhood. It's become a daily occurrence."

"Extremely possible," Dr. Miller nodded and said, "But now we need to attend to Buster, and I will need to put him under anesthesia to stitch him up. So leave Buster to me, and he'll be good as new tomorrow. You can see the receptionist, and she'll give you a time to pick Buster up."

Mrs. Hastings thanked the doctor and said goodbye to her beloved boxer with a kiss and a tear. She was heading out the door and observed an assistant pick up Buster and move him deeper into the hospital.

ᴋ ᴋ ᴋ ᴋ ᴋ ᴋ ᴋ ᴋ ᴋ ᴋ ᴋ ᴋ ᴋ ᴋ ᴋ ᴋ ᴋ ᴋ ᴋ ᴋ

The two vultures had looked as if they were circling aimlessly, but they were not. From experience they knew if they followed the major highways and the I-5 freeway, eventually, they would run across an unfortunate being that had been clipped or struck by a car. It was inevitable.

They had now drifted throughout the southern end of Orange County. As they went a little further north, they picked up the scent of decay and knew there was food ahead. Meat. It was all they thought about anymore. They had to keep eating. It was all that mattered to them.

They spied what their nose had smelled. Off the highway and just into the brush laid a large jackrabbit. Whether it was struck by a car or killed by another animal was unimportant, it was meat. This would have been too fresh for most vultures, but these two were starving. They began circling their descent toward the body while checking the surrounding area for other predators who might be lurking nearby.

The coast seemed clear, and nothing was around the body. The vultures saw a red-tailed hawk circling above them, but guessed it was looking for something fresher. Hawks would only scavenge if there were nothing else to find, which was rare for them. After several minutes the vultures landed on the rabbit and began tearing at its already damaged flesh.

As hungry as they were, the two birds knew this meal would be insufficient to satisfy them, but it would allow them to keep going. As they sliced bites of meat from the carcass they saw a shadow move over them. Suddenly the hawk also was on the rabbit, and they knew the bird didn't plan to share.

Despite the posturing and protestations of the two vultures, the hawk tightened its grip on the remains with its sharp talons and flew off with the rest of their food. It wasn't much for the hawk, but it would sustain it for another day or two. Hungry as these vultures were, they knew they were no match for the predator. They had no choice and flew off again to find a replacement meal.

The resident shorebirds of Laguna Beach were feeling the effects of their run-in with the migrating gulls. Their need for food now became the most vital thought in their minds. They began to be less patient for their next meal and often snatched anything with meat from people, both on the streets or at the beach.

One tern ambushed a couple at a restaurant just as the waiter delivered their lunch. They were so shocked as the tern grabbed the majority of their food before they could react. The restaurant owner was horrified and offered the couple not only a fresh lunch but a quiet table inside the restaurant in which to eat in peace.

More crows were hanging around, too. Even the pigeons seemed to be less afraid and more aggressive toward tourists. Killdeer and plovers that never came close to people were now after the same scraps as other birds. It became impossible to have a quiet picnic on the beach without birds interfering. Worse, each day brought more birds scavenging anything they could find.

The gulls finally found what they were searching for off Bee Canyon access road in Irvine. They could see the cloud of birds even before they saw the landfill itself. The Frank R. Bowerman landfill received 8,500 tons of waste per day. Giant bulldozers were moving mountains of material around as the gulls headed directly for the largest concentration of birds. They knew the pickings would be lushest in that area.

The gulls flew in and began sorting through the piles of discards in search of any type of meat. It was difficult, and nearly any morsel was fought over by the numerous gulls and crows searching for similar scraps. Often the gulls broke into fights where their sharp beaks would scratch or cut one another.

As the infected migrating gulls were more aggressive than any other, most of these skirmishes ended in their favor. Sometimes with an injury to other bird, sometimes not. Even with the tons of trash before them, they had trouble locating enough food to appease their appetite. More meat was needed to satisfy their craving.

They had trouble finding anything else up to that point that would have provided what the landfill offered. So they stayed and moved through the large area looking for more sustenance. They spent most of the rest of that day searching for enough food to carry them forward. Before they left, the migrating birds infected numerous resident gulls along with many of the ravens and crows at the landfill.

Though they had lost one of their kind to the falcon, the gulls picked up several more birds to add to their number. This included an errant herring gull that was much further south than it would typically have been. Similar in size and markings to the California gull, this gull species normally flourished in Alaska and was also heading north.

The herring gull decided to hitch a ride along with the

California gulls as they were heading the same direction. Including this gull, the squabble now neared twenty from its original dozen. Each one was infected with SARV.

The flock of gulls left Irvine and now flew north by northwest toward Huntington Beach and Fountain Valley. They saw a lot of people and dogs, but nothing that interested them for food. They were having great difficulty balancing their urge for food with their desire to make it to their breeding grounds.

They would generally have been deep into Los Angeles County by now instead of coming to its border. But the continued craving for meat was becoming stronger. The sun moved closer to the horizon, and they would soon stop for the day. They headed back toward the coast as they felt safer floating in the water than nesting for the night on the ground.

That same evening in central Canada where the sun had already set, another bird was on the move. Under cover of darkness, the Wilson's Phalarope, a bird not much bigger than a robin, would begin its southerly migration. They would stay in the Mono Lake until their young were raised and they had put on more than twice their weight in order to accomplish their 3,000-mile journey to South America.

It would only take an incredible three days to reach their winter grounds, primarily in Ecuador. They would reside there with the thousands of flamingos that lived in the brackish lakes. In June, the next year, the phalaropes would return to middle and southern Canada and the isolated lakes where they would breed once more.

At any one time between the Wilson's Phalarope and their cousins, the Red-necked Phalarope, over one hundred fifty thousand of these birds would summer in the Mono Lake area before traveling throughout the Western Hemisphere.

Now that the sun was not quite so bright, the coyote came out of his hiding place. Saliva was drooling from his mouth, and his head raged with pain. But he still had only one thought in his head. He needed meat, and he needed it now.

Even though the infection ravaged his body and brain, the coyote was as stealthy and sly as he had always been. This was no time to scare off any potential prey while he was this ravenous. So as he moved into the residential neighborhood where the raccoons had been before him, he stuck close to the bushes and the high ground cover along the houses.

He wasn't interested in the trash of the neighborhood. He was after something he knew would satiate his appetite much better. He picked a house on a corner with lots of bushes in the front and the field just behind it. He crouched low to the edge and waited. It wasn't long.

One of the residents was out walking her miniature dachshund as she did every day at this hour. She was about a quarter mile from her house and was heading back as she knew her dog was tiring. She walked farther than usual this day as she was still waiting for the dog to do its "business." At long last, the dog paused and began sniffing around a particular piece of turf. It finally had its movement, and the owner pulled out the little bag she had been carrying for the occasion.

With her back toward the dog, she bent over to pick up the little pile. As she did this, she loosened her grip on the leash. In that same moment, the coyote saw its chance and flew out of the bushes grabbing the dachshund by the neck and pulled the lead out of her hand. It raced to the field while the dachshund yelped in fear and pain.

The lady screamed and began frantically searching for her phone. When she found it, she quickly called 911 and reported a coyote attack and that the animal had her dog. She began moving toward the brush but came to the realization that she had nothing to defend herself with if she came upon the animal and her dog. She stood there and cried out of frustration and fear.

As soon as the coyote was in deep enough to avoid detection, it took the time to end the dog's noise making. It tore at the animal with a viciousness it had never shown before. As ruthless as coyotes can be in their pursuit of game, this went well beyond normal predation. This canine was possessed.

Animal control and a police car pulled up fifteen minutes later and spoke to the woman. The two civil servants told the woman to wait there, and they would see if they could locate her dog. Both knew that the animal would in all probability be dead, but they might catch the offending animal and take care of it before it could grab another pet.

They picked up the trail of blood that leaked from the dog's wounds and came up to an area that had a pool of blood in the grass. There was no sign of the dog's remains or its attacker, except a few pieces of fur and the lead with a ripped collar attached to it.

"Damn coyotes," said the deputy sheriff. "Every year they get bolder and more brutal."

The animal control officer was looking closely at the grass and was moving it around with his pen. "This might be a bigger problem than just an emboldened coyote. I see saliva that doesn't look normal."

He stood up and said to the officer, "Do me a favor, I need to get a specimen dish back at the truck. Stay here so I can find this spot again."

The deputy nodded and pulled his revolver, "But if you hear this go off, you better bring a bag for the rest of the coyote."

When the officer returned several minutes later, he scooped as much of the bloody saliva as he could find off the brush. "Crap, I really hope I am wrong, but I'll bet this animal has rabies based on this," he said as he looked at the specimen dish. "I have seen saliva like this before, and it almost always is."

"Great," said the deputy, "that makes it even more

important to get this thing. Should we venture deeper in? I can call this in and get a couple more officers down here to help."

"What I can't figure is where are the dog's remains?" answered the control officer. "It's is like he swallowed the dog whole, which would be impossible, even for a small dog like that. I can't see anything outside of this immediate spot. Obviously, this is where he killed the dog. The collar and lead make that plain. I don't get it."

"By the way," asked the deputy, "what did you tell the owner?"

The officer just shrugged and said, "I told her we were still looking. I didn't want to be held up any longer than I needed to get back here."

"I suppose I better tell her to go home, as she won't be walking her dog back this evening," said the deputy.

"Speaking of, it is starting to get dark, and I don't think it would be a great idea to go strolling through this brush with a potentially rabid coyote prowling the area."

"Once I report this, we will be on the lookout for him," said the deputy. "Hopefully we'll get him before it shows its face in the open again."

"Well, I for one wouldn't count on it," said the officer. "Coyotes are smart and sneaky whether rabid or not. I will come back here tomorrow and see if I can pick up his trail. Maybe I'll get lucky, and he'll be sleeping off the effects of that poor animal he killed."

"I would be careful, especially if it's as dangerous as you said," the deputy replied, "I wish you luck and good hunting, literally."

The two men walked back to give the lady the bad

news.

Officer Tom Dodge was with the San Clemente –
Dana Point Animal Services Authority. He had been
with them for many years and had dealt with every type
of animal native to the area, wild or domestic. He'd had
run-ins with rattlesnakes, skunks, raccoons, and coyotes,
to name a few.

Rabid animals were particularly troublesome to deal
with for a few reasons. Besides being potentially deadly
through the transmission of their disease, they were also
extremely aggressive, unpredictable, and never acted like
their usual behavior after the illness took effect. Dodge
had already been through the rabies vaccinations but
was wary of these animals anyway.

Many people who thought animals like raccoons were
so cute and cuddly thought much differently after being
bit by one and having to go through a series of rabies
shots, as he had.

The next morning the animal control officer returned.
He had his gun with him and sample cases. He also wore
protective gloves in case the animal surprised him and
tried to bite him. He wasn't sure if this was a good idea
or not, as the gloves prevented him from grabbing his
gun or taser in a hurry if needed. He hoped he was faster
than he thought he was.

He was asked by his department chief if he needed
help or would like the deputy sheriffs to accompany him.
He thought there was no reason for a bunch of people to

either stand around or, more likely, interfere with his search until he found the offending animal, himself.

Plus, Dodge had a list of other calls and his time searching was limited that morning. If he didn't find the animal quickly, it would have to wait for a more thorough search the following day.

He returned to the spot where the dachshund met its end and again looked for a possible cache where the coyote would return for the carcass. Seeing nothing, he looked for traces of blood or other signs that might have been left behind. Again, he had no luck.

Dodge took off his cap and scratched his head. He thought that while the dog was small, and the coyote probably hungry enough, he still could not imagine that the remains had disappeared entirely. His radio crackled, and the voice on the other side reminded him of his next appointment.

The coyote had done what Dodge thought it couldn't. In its extended stomach was all that remained of the dog. The coyote returned to its hiding place where it could avoid the sun and keep its eyes closed against the searing pain in its head. It wasn't hiding so much as it just wanted to be left alone in its misery.

CHAPTER THREE

San Clemente, San Juan Capistrano, and the surrounding areas were still in mourning. The morgue, mortuaries, and funeral parlors were filled with bodies. They worked every day and well into the evening trying to help families tend to their deceased relatives.

The victims had come from the attacks at the high school, the train, the church lot and the brutal attack at the pier. More followed from random attacks that occurred on the beaches and streets. By the time the vaccine was introduced, they were too far gone for it to have an effect. All were in temporary resting places until their final arrangements could be carried out.

More than five hundred people succumbed to the bird attacks or the disease that followed. Each one had to be attended to, and the waiting list for services seemed endless. It didn't help that the cemeteries and memorials gardens could not keep up the needed pace of burials and were having space issues of their own. Numerous complaints surfaced daily, as did stories about how families could not adequately tend to their "dead."

Residents of communities were so grief-stricken that many could not imagine coming back to any form of normality in the future. People who had received the vaccine were thankful to be alive, like Natalie Forrester, but they also felt terrible for all the families who had lost children, parents or relatives, and friends.

Some people moved away fearing that this was a temporary reprieve from the birds and that it could all begin again. While there was nothing to suggest this, they decided it was safer to find a new area. Others had lost family members and moved away to either lessen the memories or, in the case of minors, because they had lost their parents and had no other guardians nearby.

Those that were attacked, and lived, still carried the scars. The areas of the injury were inflamed and always seemed to itch. Several of the survivors went back to their doctors complaining of continually needing to scratch the area, and some had done so to the point of tearing the skin around it.

The medical community prescribed salves and ointments or recommended hydrocortisone creams, which helped alleviate the irritation for a time, but never fully cured the problem. Doctors thought it might be a form of psoriasis from an abnormal immune reaction either from the injury or possibly from the treatment.

Some of their patients also complained about another seemingly unrelated issue. They were getting cranky and out of sorts more often. Many of them said they would get angry for no apparent reason and that many things they never bothered about now annoyed them to the point of distraction. Some of them even said they felt a wave of irrational anger at times.

Most of the doctors blamed their state of mind on all the horrible happenings to them and other residents around town. Some said there was a pallor around the entire community. They thought that with time their moods, like their wounds, would heal. In extreme cases, their doctors would prescribe "a little something" to keep their anger issues at bay.

The next couple of days brought numerous changes. Many of the birds that had been in contact with the migratory gulls from San Clemente were feeling the effects of SARV on their bodies and in their heads. This included the gulls they fed with at Laguna Beach and the birds from the landfill.

In Irvine, it was primarily the crows that initially felt the effects of the virus. They already were avoiding any water, and their appetites increased. What was different about their behavior was they were socializing with as many birds as possible, regardless of species.

They flew from one side of the landfill to the other. Pecking at a few birds, but mostly rubbing their bodies against any bird, they could get close or around. They offered food they had located to the gulls and other bird species hanging around the dump with them.

The migratory gulls seemed to have a renewed purpose. While they were still continuously looking for food, they seemed to be on a desperate mission to get to their grounds at Mono Lake. They stopped any time food was available to them, and almost lost a couple of their number trying to feed on road kills that were too close to the road. If it hadn't been for the sheer number of them, cars might not have seen them in time and would not have been able to swerve and avoid the flock.

The gulls had moved up through Los Angeles County

past Santa Monica. They followed a large concentration of other gulls to a landfill in Agoura Hills. As they did in Irvine, they ate as much as they could and spent much of the day communing with these birds even though they felt pulled to continue north.

Buster had returned home all stitched up and with a cone around his neck to keep him from bothering the doctor's good work. That alone was enough to upset him, but he wasn't feeling like himself at all. He was off his kibble that he used to love and wasn't drinking any water, either. His owners used to complain about the mess at the water bowl Buster always made.

Now they wished he would. They began to get concerned about their pet and made another appointment after describing their concerns. When they met with Dr. Miller again, she looked carefully at the stitches.

The wound was inflamed, and she figured the injury was infected. The dog's temperature was also elevated which further suggested this. She prescribed antibiotics for Buster and indicated that the dog may be off its food and water because of the infection, and hopefully, this medicine would resolve the issue in a couple days.

She asked Buster's owners to give the office a follow-up call in a day or two and let them know.

Even though it had only been less than a couple weeks since the raccoons had stumbled across the dead vulture. They already were responding like an animals who had rabies for a couple months or longer. Like the coyote, they were drooling, choking and frothing at the mouth due to their throats constricting from the virus.

They also moved slower and had lost part of the agility in their legs. They continued on the prowl, looking for any type of meat. What was the most alarming was their heightened aggression. They snapped and growled at anything that moved, even the breeze.

Raccoons are always a threat in the wild with standard mammalian rabies, but this strain of disease made matters much worse. The infection spread faster and was far more aggressive than the worst case of mammalian rabies. Already the coyote and the raccoons were at the stage that regular mammalian rabies would be after several weeks.

The locals were getting their fill from the constant raids on their garbage and attempts of aggression toward their animals and children. A few had seen the bandits roaming through the neighborhood and had reported their activities to animal control. Trucks would roll by from the department, but they weren't able to catch sight of the raccoons during their patrols. The cat and mouse game continued without resolve each new day.

ᛌ ᛌᛐᛌ ᛌ ᛌᛐᛌ ᛌ ᛌᛐᛌ ᛌ ᛌᛐ ᛌ ᛌᛐᛌ ᛌ ᛌᛐᛌ ᛌ ᛌᛐᛌ

Buster showed no improvement, and like the raccoons

and coyote, was feeling the ravages of the disease on his body and mind. He wanted meat, and his owners kept pushing dry food at him. They kept shoving him toward that horrible water bowl, and he wanted nothing at all to do with that.

They called the veterinarian's office and reported that Buster just wasn't himself anymore and that he would not eat or drink, and was beginning to growl and snap at them. They were afraid to approach him with the medicine as he was very aggressive. They were asked if they could bring him in and let Dr. Miller look at him.

Buster really did not want to go anywhere and was trying to hide under a lamp table that was too small for him. Mr. Hastings had stayed home from work to attend to his dog and walked over to place the lead on him. As he attached the hook onto the collar, the dog attempted to bite him, which he had never done before. If it hadn't been for the cone around Buster's neck, he would have succeeded at grabbing Mr. Hastings arm.

They had to drag Buster into the car and tie him down with the lead. The dog was snapping at everything around him, hoping to latch on to something or someone. When they got him to the vet, Mr. Hastings again had to drag the dog into the office. Buster growled and threatened the other animals waiting their turn to see the doctor. Mr. Hastings had his hands full trying to calm his dog without getting in the way of those teeth.

When they finally got into the inner office, Dr. Miller took one look at Buster and told her assistant to put Buster in a cage in the back immediately. The Hastings, already distraught over their dog's behavior just looked at the vet with questioning eyes.

"What's wrong with him?" asked Mrs. Hastings, tears starting to well in her eyes.

"I can't know how this happened, but I am convinced that Buster is rabid," said Dr. Miller. "I can't believe it, and this is the shortest incubation period I have ever heard of, but I am convinced whatever gave Buster his wounds gave him rabies as well."

"But he is up on all his shots, including his rabies vaccination." protested Mr. Hastings.

"I am at a loss as well, but I have seen my share of rabid animals over the years, and he is exhibiting several classic signs, including partial paralysis in his hind legs, which is why you had to drag him in here, and why we had to do the same just now. That plus the excessive drool and frothing are clinical signs of rabies."

"What's going to happen to him? Can you cure him?" cried Mrs. Hastings.

"I am afraid that if my prognosis is confirmed, we will have to put Buster down," Dr. Miller said as delicately as possible. "Once rabies takes effect, it is impossible to cure. Plus he is now a risk to any person or animal near him."

"You still haven't told us how this could happen?" said Mr. Hastings. "I was under the impression once inoculated, he could not get rabies."

Dr. Miller was at a loss over this, herself. This shouldn't have happened. "Unless there is a new strain of rabies or something, I can't tell you, either. But I promise I will look into it." She turned her attention to the Hastings, and asked them, "Now, and this is important, did either of you get bit or scratched by Buster?"

Mr. Hastings said, "He tried to bite me but luckily that cone thing got in the way, and he couldn't reach me."

Mrs. Hastings still crying shook her head.

"Well thank goodness for that," responded the doctor, "You would have been in for a terrible time if you had. I will observe Buster for the rest of the day and have the office call you tomorrow with the results."

By now, the vet was anxious to learn more about the situation before her. She was impatient to check the information from the CDC to see if Buster's maladies coincided with the notice she knew was on her office wall. She already knew what had to be done but wasn't about to tell the Hastings what the procedure entailed.

The couple was reluctant to go without more information, but it was clear they had been dismissed. The Hastings thanked the doctor and left the inner exam room.

The moment they were gone the doctor went in and looked into the murderous eyes of Buster who laid in his cage growling softly. She stood up and looked at the notice on the wall about immediately reporting bird attacks on people to the CDC. She knew no bird tore up Buster's hind end like that, but what if he was attacked by another animal, and that animal was rabid from a bird?

She thought about how Mrs. Hastings complained about how raccoons were hanging around their trash. Birds and raccoons often share meals. What if the bird attacked the raccoon, or more likely, the raccoon attacked and killed the bird? Maybe the bird infected the raccoon with the new super aviary rabies, who in turn infected Buster?

The notice stated that SARV was a new strain of rabies with unusual properties. But she had heard before that all the birds with the virus died off which poked a big hole in her theory.

Dr. Miller decided the only way to know was to carry out the procedure as mandated by the State of California. There was no accurate way to test a dog that is alive for rabies. The rabies virus cannot be verified through the bloodstream because it travels through the nervous system from the original transmission bite to the brain. Mammalian rabies also enters the salivary glands, but current saliva testing isn't 100 percent accurate.

She had to euthanize Buster and then decapitate him and send the head to the lab for rabies testing. This was the only way to positively test for rabies, whether mammalian or the new aviary strain.

CHAPTER FOUR

The vultures moved from one dead body to the next. They were never able to satiate their constant hunger. It did not matter if it was freshly killed or hardly anything left, they had to try and get as much as possible to fill their seemingly empty stomachs.

One of the vultures even attempted to take a freshly dead cottontail from a large diamondback rattlesnake. The snake almost bit the vulture twice before the bird decided to fly off.

The good news was the vultures left nothing behind except a few bones and some fur or feathers. Not even enough for mice or voles to bother with. They had drifted north well into central Orange County and were hovering around Laguna Niguel and Mission Viejo neighborhoods looking for anything to eat.

ᕏᕁᕏ ᕏᕁᕏᕁᕏ ᕏᕁᕏᕁᕏ ᕁᕏ ᕏᕁᕏᕁᕏ ᕏᕁᕏᕁ ᕏᕁᕏᕁ

For the second day since the dachshund was taken, Officer Dodge went out again in an attempt to find the coyote that grabbed the resident's pet. He knew that saliva testing wasn't accurate, but suspected the sample he'd submitted would come back positive for rabies. He hoped to get the verification that day.

Dodge returned to the place he'd been called to two evenings prior. This time Dodge took his loop snare along with his taser and revolver. He marched once more through the brush to the area where they had found what little remained of the dog. He looked around again, trying to figure where the coyote might have gone to rest.

After looking around the brush again for possible clues, he stood up and chose the most likely direction the coyote would have gone. Dodge headed deeper into the brush toward a stand of trees, which was his guess. There was still no sign of either the coyote or its prey. The brush seemed undisturbed, and he still could not spot a single drop of blood.

When he reached the trees, the brush had thinned out, and Dodge began checking for possible hiding places or dug-out areas that the coyote might use for shelter. He found one possibility at the third tree he reached. There was a shallow den-like area with fresh dirt dug under a large root of the tree.

But no coyote.

He continued his search creeping as softly as possible so as not to spook his quarry if it was near. He would be no match for a foot race with a coyote and knew it. He approached another large tree toward the end of the clearing. He figured it was the oldest one there as it had many long, thick and gnarled branches reaching toward the sky.

As he moved closer, he stooped lower to check around the base of the trunk. When he finally stood up straight, the coyote sprung from the branch that was even with the officer. He immediately latched onto Dodge's throat and tore it open even as the officer reached for the animal. Both Dodge and the coyote hit the ground.

One was dead, the other was not.

The Peregrine Falcon chicks were now fledged and flying around their nest with their parents. Still a little unsteady, they were learning to fashion their hunting and maneuvering skills and with good reason. They were always rapaciously hungry. As were their parents.

The two adults were chasing down and eating anything they could come close to catching. The male killed a large tomcat and ate a good portion right there on the spot. The remains were left for whatever animal or bird came by later, including his chicks.

The parents were not feeding the chicks anymore, but they led them to available food sources they had killed. All four of the birds were consuming food at an alarming rate for any bird their size. Nothing but a few bones and some fur or feathers remained.

The disease continued to spread around Irvine.

The gulls and crows that resided at and around the Frank L. Bowerman landfill were now having an impossible time satisfying their hunger. Seventeen thousand pounds of trash were insufficient to their needs. They needed meat. Fresh, unspoiled meat.

Most of these birds had lived their entire existence at the dump. They never had to venture any further to find enough food to sustain them. They were utterly unaccustomed to traveling outside the area. Even during breeding, gulls made their nest from scrapes in the ground just outside the borders of the landfill and raised their young off the refuse they found.

Similarly, crows made their nests in trees nearby and spent the majority of their foraging in the same area. Many crows had removed shiny objects during their undertakings and decorated their nest with them. But now they ignored anything that wasn't meat.

It was still early in the morning, but the different types of birds were already flying together in the search for something that could fulfill the perversion from their regular diet. They watched the massive bulldozers below them. These giant machines were nearly two stories tall and moved thousands of pounds of trash throughout the landfill. The operators of these behemoths were well protected inside them.

The birds hovered around the offices and watched the first of the trash trucks and semi-trailers bringing in tons of new refuse. Several people were moving around these areas coming and going as quickly as they could. But they were always with others as they emptied their loads and then left.

Something happened that caught their attention. One of the bulldozers had stopped working. It was quiet in the middle of the area the driver had been working on. They saw the person in the cab exit the yellow monster and examine the now defunct machine.

After several minutes, he began walking in the direction of the place where the other people were with their trucks. But currently he was alone and quite a distance from the others.

The first crow hit his helmet and knocked it off the man's head. A gull hit his back as he bent over to pick it up and nearly knocked the man down. Another crow hit his head again before the man could replace the protective gear.

Then another gull and another struck the man. He spun around suddenly trying to protect his head and face. A different crow, followed by a raven, struck him from his other side. No one from the landfill noticed the man fighting off the ever-growing onslaught of the birds. They were quite used to seeing flocks of birds concentrating on a particular area when something of interest was discovered.

The man fell to his knees attempting to make himself a smaller target and more difficult to hit. The birds saw it as a weakness and escalated their attack. Soon the man was covered with birds, and as he screamed out, the beaks dove for any exposed flesh they could reach.

The heavy jeans and boots protected most of his lower body, but his upper body was either clothed in a thin t-shirt or exposed. Ten minutes later the man's face resembled something that had been through a meat grinder. His hands and arms were also shredded to the bones and blood leaked from attacks through his shirt.

It was about two hours later before they discovered the body. No one had the faintest clue as to what happened. The birds had left the scene of the crime and had flown to the other side of the fill.

Deputy sheriffs were called in to investigate. As they

examined the corpse, they were able to accurately surmise what took place from previous events they heard about in San Clemente. Not long after, word was going through the sheriff's department. This was followed by a call to Dr. Anna Lanz at the CDC and a subsequent call to Dr. Bill Forrester's office at UCSD.

The birds were at it again. Once more, the triumvirate was on high alert.

"Irvine, really?" Dr. Forrester asked on his phone. "Did anyone witness the attack? Oh, I see. I am sorry. Yes, my assistant and I will get there as soon as we can."

As Dr. Forrester ended the call, he turned to Tory and said, "We were wrong. This is not over. We just had another bird attack, and it was fatal."

ʞ ʞ ⱦ ʞ ʞ ⱦ ʞ ʞ ⱦ ʞ ⱦ ʞ ʞ ⱦ ʞ ʞ ⱦ ʞ ʞ ⱦ

As Dr. Lanz told her assistant to call Dr. Forrester at UCSD, she was dialing her own phone. She heard it connect.

"This is Alice Friedman," the phone answered.

"Dr. Friedman, we just had another fatality, and the sheriff's office believes it was done by birds," Dr. Lanz said in one long breath.

"In San Clemente?" asked Dr. Friedman.

"Unfortunately, no. This happened at a landfill in Irvine," Lanz answered.

"Anywhere near the train station?" Dr. Friedman was thinking fast as she began gathering up things from her desk.

"It is about seven miles from there," replied Dr. Lanz.

"We already looked at that, and that's by car, it might be less as the crow flies, no pun intended."

"Irvine is quite a ways from San Clemente if I remember," Dr. Friedman said thinking out loud.

"From the landfill to the pier is almost thirty miles," said Dr. Lanz.

"That's farther than any attack we heard about before. The furthest victim we had before was from Santa Ana, but she was attacked at the beach in San Clemente," said Dr. Friedman.

"Is it possible a bird that was infected got away at the Irvine station and didn't die-off with the others?" asked Dr. Lanz.

"I guess that could be possible, as the birds killed there were shot or bludgeoned and didn't die naturally," said Dr. Friedman. "Maybe one or two escaped and were hanging around the landfill. But why haven't we heard of an attack sooner? And I would have guessed they would have died off by now like the others. We already know how fast this strain of rabies works. Something doesn't gel."

"I assume you will be returning to California?" asked Dr. Lanz.

"I have been packing my desk while we talked," said Dr. Friedman. "I will arrange a plane as soon as I hang up, and I want a full briefing when I arrive. Luckily you are three hours behind us, so I should get there by late afternoon."

"Call me when you have an ETA, and I'll be there to meet you. We should know more, and I will fill you in then," said Dr. Lanz. "Sorry to cut your stay at home so short, but I'll see you, soon." They said goodbye, and she hit end on her phone.

ᴋ ᴋᵗᴋ ᴋ ᴋᵗᴋ ᴋ ᴋᵗᴋ ᴋ ᴋᵗ ᴋ ᴋᵗᴋ ᴋ ᴋᵗᴋ ᴋ ᴋᵗᴋ

The sheriff's office in San Clemente was also busy tending to the remains of Officer Dodge and searching for a rabid coyote.

When Dodge's sample came back as positive for rabies, they tried contacting him on the radio. When he didn't respond after several attempts, they sent a sheriff's car out to investigate. The deputy found the animal control truck where Dodge parked it and began searching the area calling his name.

Unlike the coyote, Dodge had parted the brush and left a fairly easy trail to follow. When the deputy came to the clearing with the trees, he could see what was left of Dodge by the big tree. It was a grisly sight, as the coyote tore up the animal control officer and did not leave much behind.

Other deputies were now on the scene and hunting the coyote with malice for their fallen brethren. Most had worked with Tom Dodge in the past, and everyone liked him. Some of the deputies could not believe only one animal did this. One of the deputies became sick at the site of the corpse.

It was difficult removing Dodge's remains, but the attendees from the coroner's office had become used to scenes like this in San Clemente. They had hoped to have seen the last, but apparently not.

In all, ten deputies were combing the brush and

residences from the area. The coyote had left a blood trail as he moved away from the body, but soon it faded to nothing, and they couldn't follow it through the thick brush with any certainty.

It turned out the coyote had moved toward the other side of the neighborhood and was disoriented as it stepped out onto the road. It was immediately struck by a car and killed. One of the deputies heard the squeal of brakes and heard a car hit something. He radioed in immediately and called for back-up to his location.

He ran out of the brush as the lady was about to reach down and check the animal she had run over.

"Get away from that thing!" he yelled to her.

The deputy had drawn his revolver in case the coyote was alive. He approached the animal and saw it was dead. He apologized to the women, explaining that the animal was infected with rabies. He waited at the spot until another animal control truck arrived and helped load the body for testing and disposal.

What Dodge never learned was the report that came back showed a type of rabies, but not the common disease found in mammals. Since saliva tests were inconclusive, they chalked it up as anomalies from the field test, itself.

They would learn more now that they had the head for examination.

ᛕᛕᛕᛕ ᛕᛕᛕᛕ ᛕᛕᛕᛕᛕᛕ ᛕᛕᛕᛕᛕᛕᛕ ᛕᛕᛕᛕ

Dr. Forrester and Tory were throwing items in the car that they used the last time they were after rabid birds.

They had cages, nets, snares, heavy gloves and vaccine vials. Dr. Forrester had called Natalie and asked her to pack a bag for a few nights as they would probably have to remain in Irvine.

Dr. Forrester stopped at his home to retrieve his bags and say goodbye to his wife. He told Tory to wait in the car as he would be but a moment. As he entered the door, he had one of his overnight bags thrown at him by Natalie.

"I hope you and your trollop enjoy your little getaway," she seethed.

"What's that for, Nat?" he looked at her completely baffled by her anger.

"You think I am so stupid, don't you? Like I don't know what's going on. You spend more time with that student than you ever do with me. I am fed up with it," yelled Natalie.

"You know why I have had to spend so much time at the lab. And now we have another crisis with these birds. I have no choice but to go, and I need Tory to help get everything sorted out. You have never been jealous or concerned before. You have always known better. Please don't start now," Dr. Forrester pleaded.

Dr. Forrester picked up his bag and headed for the door. "Goodbye, Nat. We can discuss this further when I get back." He turned and walked out the door. He heard something crash against the door as he left.

Dr. Forrester drove Tory to her apartment where she packed a bag and grabbed some essentials for herself. He remained in the car replaying his wife's words and actions in his mind. He and Natalie never fought or said harsh words to each other. Something was terribly wrong.

In less than ten minutes Tory left her apartment and was back in Dr. Forrester's car. He hit the gas, and they were speeding their way toward Irvine.

"Do you think these are the same birds from San Clemente?" asked Tory.

"I can't imagine. How could they live so much longer than all the other birds?" questioned Dr. Forrester.

"It has only been about a week since the die-off, perhaps they were infected at the end and are just showing signs now," Tory said.

"It doesn't seem possible that these are birds from the train attack," said Forrester. "We were unable to find one bird even half dead. Everything we collected was shot or beat to a pulp. None of the witnesses said any birds escaped."

"Maybe one did. That is all it would take. Let's not forget it was a dead cockatoo that started all this in the first place," said Tory.

"Now that you mention it, maybe we missed a bird in the clean-up, and another non-infected bird got to it," said Dr. Forrester.

"We know that is what started spreading the infection in San Clemente with that vulture," Tory reminded him.

"I was hoping we would have the antivirus perfected before this could happen again. Looks like we were too optimistic," said Dr. Forrester.

"We still haven't come up with a solution on how to administer it, even if we did have it ready," Tory sighed.

Dr. Forrester shrugged, "First things, first.

Apparently, we have another chance to get a live specimen to try it out on."

Tory thought for a moment and then asked, "Since the disease spreads so quickly, do you think it is possible to capture a bird early enough in the stages of the disease to cure it?"

"I've wondered about that myself. Talking to Ellen Revere, she said the disease infected the mice she tested almost overnight. This is a mean virus," said Dr. Forrester. "I believe things are about to get a whole lot worse."

ʞ ʇ↑ʇ ʞ ʇ↑ʇ ʞ ʇ↑ʇ ʇ↑ ʞ ʇ↑ʇ ʞ ʇ↑ʇ ʞ ʇ↑ʇ

The last of the Eared Grebes were flying into Mono Lake. This bird was larger than the Red-necked Phalarope and a little smaller than a mallard. It had a pointed beak that it used to catch insects and brine shrimp that were available by the trillions in Mono Lake.

They were called "Eared" Grebes for the beautiful golden feathers that extended from behind their brilliant red eyes. Their body resembled a duck but without the webbed feet or flattened bill. They could be seen diving and swimming underwater for food. These gregarious birds always flocked together, especially during breeding season, which was currently taking place at Mono Lake.

The Eared Grebes were one of five species of grebes that frequented the area. With these birds coming into the area, it brought the total population of Eared Grebes at Mono Lake to 1.8 million birds, which represented 51 percent of the entire species.

Within two hours of the call, the plane was in the air with Dr. Friedman and several others from the CDC that had experience from San Clemente during the last attack. The flight was a government charter, so Friedman had no problem talking on the satellite phone while in flight.

She was talking to a man from Homeland Security and coordinating a pick-up time when he arrived from Washington, D.C., shortly after her. She spoke to him before, the day after the die-off. He made it impeccably clear that if any instances resurfaced with the birds, he was to be at the top of her short list to be notified.

Dr. Grant Abernathy was also on the plane coordinating extended stay hotels and setting up a new command center at UCI Medical Center. There was no reason to return to Saddleback in San Clemente as the problem moved north into Irvine. Plus this facility was larger and more complex than the other. He feared he would need all that and more this time.

By now the migrating California gulls made it to Point Magu in Ventura County. They alighted near the naval air station there and fed on another concentration of small fish. Still driven continuously by hunger, they knew they were making headway toward their final goal, even if much slower than usual. At their current rate, it would take nearly another seven or eight days to reach their destination. Usually, they would have made the entire trip by this time. But the birds had to hunt anything they thought they could catch or find, which slowed them considerably.

They had feasted on a couple schools of fish along the way with other shorebirds. They even found the remains of a dead deer near the coastal highway they flew along. It had already been scavenged by other animals in the area, but the remains still afforded them something to help tide their incredible appetites. They had stripped the deer to its bones and left little behind for anything else. Their savagery scared away any other animals thinking of trying to feed with the birds.

The seabirds were still pushed by their desire to get to their Mono Lake haven and their hunger for the food that awaited them there. Once they arrived, they would join the roughly 75,000 California Gulls that inhabited the area for the summer and fall.

There they would be cohabitants with the other ten gull and tern species, including Herring and Bonaparte's Gulls, Black and Common Terns, and many more.

ㄍ ㄍ⁺ㄍ ㄍ ㄍ⁺ㄍ ㄍ ㄍ⁺ㄍ ㄍ⁺ㄍ ㄍ ㄍ⁺ㄍ ㄍ ㄍ⁺ㄍ ㄍ ㄍ⁺ㄍ

Dr. Forrester and Tory arrived first to Irvine. They had a little difficulty locating the landfill as it wasn't publicly obvious, being strictly a commercial operation. Forrester's GPS brought them close enough for him to follow a trash truck the rest of the way to the facility.

When he arrived at the gate, the guard almost refused

entry to him. It wasn't until he threatened him with having the sheriff's deputies arrest him for interfering with a crime scene investigation that the guard relented. He drove up to one of the deputies that was still questioning the other employees and visitors and identified himself to the officer.

"Yes, I was told to expect you," the deputy said. "You are the bird guys, right?"

The comment sent a shiver down Tory's back. That was almost the identical remark that the first victim in San Clemente said to her in front of Chris. This really was all happening again.

Tory and Dr. Forrester listened to the other operators tell the deputies that the birds had always been aggressive and tried to peck them on occasion. They had never sustained a severe injury, and certainly nothing like this. Generally, they flew away to avoid the bulldozers and the thousands of pounds of refuse they pushed in front of them.

Dr. Forrester asked if they noticed any unusual gatherings of birds of different types, the question was greeted by chuckles and one operator said, "They are always flocking together here. Damn seagulls, crows, starlings, and a whole lot of birds I don't know the names of. They are always together, and in every damn place we are."

After a few more comments, Dr. Forrester guided Tory back toward his car. Forrester said. "If they are already gathering together as they did in San Clemente..."

Tory finished his thought, "...then imagine how

organized they would become in an environment like this one?"

Dr. Forrester nodded, "It also doesn't give us a clue how the birds got infected in the first place or which could be and which aren't." He looked around at all the winged creatures flying around in front of them.

"Where do we start and how could we know which are already a threat?" Tory asked.

"I think we are going to need a lot of help," Dr. Forrester said. "We need to talk to the CDC and brainstorm how to approach this. We need to capture as many of these birds as possible, and hope that any infected birds haven't flown off before we do."

Dr. Forrester knew that Dr. Friedman was already enroute to Orange County and was bringing a full staff with her. He called the number on his phone for Dr. Abernathy.

"This is Grant," Dr. Abernathy answered.

"Dr. Abernathy, this is Bill Forrester."

"Dr. Forrester, we were going to call you when we got set up. Dr. Friedman and I think we need to get together tomorrow."

"When will you be arriving?" asked Forrester.

"We touch down at around 4:30 this afternoon. We are setting up at UCI Medical," answered Dr. Abernathy.

"Can we meet this evening somewhere?" Dr. Forrester asked.

"Hold on a second," Dr. Abernathy said and talked to someone else on the jet. He came back and said, "How about 6:30 p.m. at our hotel?"

Dr. Forrester agreed and then got the details of the

hotel. He said he'd see them later and hung up.

"We better have some idea of a plan when we meet them. Because they are going to expect one," said Dr. Forrester.

"Maybe we should go check in to our hotel and do some brainstorming before we need to meet them?" asked Tory.

Dr. Forrester nodded. They got in the car and headed off.

The birds that participated in the attack on the operator were at the far end of the landfill all congregated together. Their appetite surfeited for at least the next day or more.

In San Clemente, one of the two raccoons looked as if it was having an epileptic episode. It was lying on its side with its mouth open and drool running out of it. Its back legs did not work, and its front legs were pawing the air but not grabbing anything. Its eyes had rolled back into its head as it went through its death throes.

Its partner just stood by unable to help the raccoon. This raccoon snapped at the air as if there were pests all around it. Like the raccoon on its side, the second raccoon's legs were barely working, and the frothing and drool from its mouth were as bad as the first raccoon.

Within a couple hours, both raccoons had succumbed to their disease. Neither had infected another animal or person beyond Buster before dying. Better still, they died near the street of the houses they had pillaged, and animal control was summoned before anything else could run across them.

San Clemente finally dodged a bullet.

ᛕ ᛕᛏᛕ ᛕ ᛕᛏᛕ ᛕ ᛕᛏᛕ ᛕ ᛕᛏ ᛕ ᛕᛏᛕ ᛕ ᛕᛏᛕ ᛕ ᛕᛏᛕ

The peregrines had been searching all through the neighborhood for something to eat. One of the young falcons was looking for anything that moved. It was nearly out of its mind with hunger. Plus the sun was beginning to set lower in the sky, making his hunt that much more urgent before night could fall.

It saw an old man moving slowly down a street. The young falcon took the man's slow movement as dying prey. The falcon swooped in and grabbed the man on his shoulder taking a bite of his ear with its sharp beak, ripping the lobe from the rest of the ear.

A young man approaching from the other direction saw the attack and ran up and struck the bird knocking it off the old man. The bird lay stunned for a moment, then got up and flew off before the man could do anything about it.

The old man was crying and bleeding badly from the wound he sustained and the man who helped him called 911.

An ambulance and a sheriff's deputy came to the scene, and as the young man relayed what happened, another call about a bird attack in Irvine hit the airwaves.

ᛕ ᛕᛏᛕ ᛕ ᛕᛏᛕ ᛕ ᛕᛏᛕ ᛕ ᛕᛏ ᛕ ᛕᛏᛕ ᛕ ᛕᛏᛕ ᛕ ᛕᛏᛕ

The CDC checked into the Residence Inn in Irvine around 5:45 that afternoon. Dr. Forrester and Tory entered the lobby at 6:20 p.m. and found a host of people waiting for them. They ushered the visitors into a conference room already set up with water and glasses and snack items.

Dr. Bill Forrester knew it was going to be a long night.

As they took their places, Dr. Friedman said a brief hello and then asked how they were coming along with their vaccine to counteract SARV.

They explained the problems they had because no live specimens with the disease were on hand to test the vaccine.

"Why not simply vaccinate a healthy bird and then introduce the virus afterward?" asked a man seated next to Dr. Friedman.

"The issue is the SAR virus seems to change or mutate after death. We don't know if the vaccine would be effective against the live virus," answered Dr. Forrester.

"Well, we are out of time to find out," replied the man.

"I am sorry, we haven't been introduced, I am Dr. Bill Forrester. And you are?"

The man stood up and barely cleared the people on either side of him. He only stood about five foot two inches. He appeared to be in his early to mid-sixties. He had light brown hair and deep-set hazel eyes. He had wrinkles under the eyes making it appear as if he was wearing glasses where none existed.

"My name is Dr. Henry Greenwood, and I am with Homeland Security. I am here to make sure we kill this virus once and for all, and immediately."

Dr. Forrester asked, "I may be naive, but what does Homeland Security have to do with this? And may I ask your specialty?"

"I am in Biotic Crisis, and this has now become a national and potentially international threat," Dr. Greenwood stated.

"Biotic crisis? Isn't that having to do with extinction events? Do you actually believe this has come that far?" asked Tory.

"I am afraid you do not have any idea how potentially close we are to a major extinction event. We have been looking at the numbers and the possible disaster that confronts us right this very minute," explained Dr. Greenwood. "My colleagues and I guessed before that this would not be contained in San Clemente, and I am sorry to say we were right.

"But the birds all died off," said Dr. Forrester defensively.

"Obviously not all based on these two new attacks," said Dr. Greenwood.

"Two? There was another?" asked Tory.

"About twelve miles from the landfill murder, in downtown Irvine, an elderly man was attacked and injured by what we believe was a Peregrine Falcon," said Dr. Friedman.

"The distance from the landfill incident suggests that it was unrelated as far as the same group of birds involved. This leads us to believe that birds are being infected by a bird or birds that may be on the move," said Dr. Greenwood. "This was our gravest concern."

"So you think, what? That a migrating bird is transmitting the disease?" asked Dr. Forrester.

"More likely an entire flock," answered Dr. Greenwood.

Dr. Forrester thought for a moment, and then his eyes got big.

"Ah, I see in your eyes you just started to put this together," smirked Dr. Greenwood.

"Oh my God, if they are moving up the coast, they could infect all types of birds! Especially if they are feeding or around where they can defecate. We already know that was how SARV spread before," said Dr. Forrester.

"Precisely, but it is far worse than I believe you are imagining. If they are heading to one of the major breeding grounds like say, San Francisco, Mono Lake, or the Great Salt Lake, they could potentially spread the disease through every corner of the globe, and quickly."

"And on to nearly every living thing on the planet," breathed Tory.

"Not only this but even if they kept the disease just among the birds. Imagine what would happen to our ecosystem once the birds died off," said Dr. Greenwood.

"The populations of insects, fish, and small mammals would explode. We would be overrun in a matter of years," said Dr. Forrester.

"We figure less than three if no other animals are affected, and one if, as we predict, they are," said Dr. Greenwood.

"Hence, a global extinction event," Dr. Forrester concluded.

"We have to stop this virus and whatever birds are infected today to prevent this from taking place," Dr. Greenwood placed his hands on the table and leaned as far forward toward Dr. Forrester and Tory as he was able. He spoke slowly, "So I will ask this again, how far are you and Professor Revere to providing a vaccine for the birds and animals against SARV?"

For the next two and a half hours, they talked about the experiments and their results thus far. They then came up with a possible list of birds that migrated from or through Southern California and their potential routes and destinations.

It was an exhaustive list. "The Pacific Flyway," as it is called, is used by every type of bird from shorebirds, waterfowl, songbirds, and even raptors. Hummingbird species used the flyway to move to and from their winter and summer habitats. Many species travel from South and Central America to Northern Alaska and Canada and back again.

Once these birds reach their destinations, they mingle with other bird species that crisscross east and west from the Western United States throughout the country all the way to Europe and beyond.

"We have another problem with timing," said Tory, "While it can take some birds weeks to get to their destinations, others can make the trip from South America to the Great Salt Lake in three days."

"Let's hope for our sake, that isn't the case here. If it is, we already lost the race for humanity," said Dr.

Greenwood.

"Another question is how can we possibly vaccinate every living creature before it is exposed to the rabies virus?" asked Dr. Forrester.

"The vaccine itself will have to be something that can be introduced through the air," said Dr. Abernathy, "We have been working on needle-less vaccines for flu and other health issues. This will have to be one of those."

"But that's impossible! We are still working on an injectable antivirus, and an airborne version could be years off," complained Dr. Forrester.

"We will have every medical facility at our disposal to make this work," said Dr. Friedman as she nodded to Dr. Greenwood. "And we have Homeland Security to make it happen."

Dr. Greenwood said, "Plus how can you inject millions of birds ahead of the spread of the virus? It can't be done."

"One thing is for sure," said Dr. Lanz, "If we don't make this happen, it isn't going to matter much who we work for, or what we do, because we won't be here much longer."

That one statement summed up the urgency before them. Regardless of any logistics and problems, they had only days to stop a global extinction from occurring.

CHAPTER FIVE

Professor Ellen Revere received a call from Washington, D.C., at her home by 6:30 that morning. She was requested to pack up her lab and all her research and be on a government plane to California at 9:30 that same morning. While the conversation was amiable enough, it left no question that she was being ordered by a high-ranking government official.

She knew that the van being sent to the college for her research materials and her, along with a chartered jet from Homeland Security did not leave any room for argument. She was told that she would be briefed upon arrival, but she already knew from Bill Forrester that the birds were attacking once more.

She had been working with both birds and mice testing the McKnight SAR vaccine and then injecting them with the virus following. It worked on the mice to stem the spread of the disease, but the mice were far more aggressive afterward and seemed to be scratching and grooming themselves continually.

Apparently, there were side-effects of the vaccine. Revere had a couple of lab students helping her pack, and as one student grabbed a cage to move it, he was bitten by the vaccinated mouse in it.

"Damn it!" the student cried out and almost dropped the cage before setting it down quickly.

Prof. Revere came over and examined the young man.

She now had a puzzle before her. Would she have to begin rabies treatments for her student? Or should she just treat the bite and send him on his way? She contacted the medical staff she had been working with at Cornell and was told better to be safe than sorry.

She told the student to go see the doctor she had been working with to begin the treatment. She would have seen to this herself, but she had a plane to catch. She put her protective gloves back on and moved the cage to the cart with the others.

"Just for that little fellow you are going to California," she said to the mouse. "And you better hope you aren't met by a bird or it will do worse to you."

She was thankful that it wasn't one of the infected mice. However, she knew it couldn't be, as they were already dead. They had all died in a matter of days from the rabies virus.

By 6:30 that morning in California, Dr. Forrester and Tory were setting up their lab equipment and samples at the biology department at the University of California – Irvine, or UCI, as it was known. All the strings were pulled, and before they broke up their meeting the previous evening, a truck was ordered to UCSD and Dr. Forrester's laboratories to collect anything that could be loaded and brought to Irvine.

It arrived a half hour before, and an army of people was moving everything to the lab where he now stood with Tory. The dean of the biology department had placed all of his professors and lab assistants at their disposal and offered whatever help they needed.

The campus was relatively near the Medical Center where Dr. Abernathy had set up the CDC facilities and offices. Irvine was now the host to the most vital mission and operation on the planet.

ʞ ʞ

Prof. Revere's plane touched down at 12:30 in the afternoon. She was met by the same army that had retrieved the supplies and files from San Diego, and they were unloading the plane before she could reach the car to take her to UCI.

She called back saying, "Be careful of those mice, they'll bite." Prof. Revere got into the waiting car, and it sped off.

When she arrived at the UCI campus, Tory and Dr. Forrester were waiting at the door. They embraced, and all three said how pleased they were to see each other, although the reason was regrettable. Drs. Friedman and Abernathy pulled up a moment later and greeted Prof. Revere. Dr. Friedman asked they all step into the building and head for Dr. Forrester's lab.

Once inside, Dr. Friedman said to Prof. Revere, "We have four mammals on ice in San Clemente. One coyote, one dog, and two raccoons for you to examine. They all have rabies, but not common mammalian rabies. It may be our SARV variety. I am getting their heads sent over for you to look at."

"I would be surprised if it is," said Prof. Revere. "The

SARV spreads far too quickly for it to incubate that long since the die-off. I lost seven mice within a couple days. Although these animals are larger than mice, we know they would not last long with the same virus."

"I don't know if I want to believe it is or not," said Dr. Friedman. "In some ways that would tie it together nicely, but mostly I am concerned that would mean SARV is spreading into the animal kingdom which scares me, greatly."

Dr. Forrester said, "Plus it would also mean we are not finished in San Clemente if it is SARV. Meaning we are back to fighting on multiple fronts."

They told Prof. Revere about the bulldozer operator and the old man that were the latest victims of the birds.

"We may have some good news about the suspected falcon," announced Dr. Abernathy. "It seems there is a nest of peregrines at the top of the building where the poor old guy was attacked. We think the birds are still hanging around it."

"That's incredible!" yelled Tory.

Prof. Revere laughed at her saying, "I sure hope I get used to that exuberance you are always displaying, Tory."

Dr. Forrester shook his head saying, "I never have."

Then more seriously Prof. Revere said, "We need to go up there with some nets and see if we can catch one or more of these birds, which I am sure won't be easy."

Dr. Friedman shook her head and said, "I think it is more important for you three to continue working on an antivirus that can be administered. I have plenty of boots on the ground that can catch birds. Your job is to cure them, or better still, make sure they don't get infected in the first place."

The three nodded, and Prof. Revere said, "I guess we have our marching orders."

Just as Drs. Friedman and Abernathy left, Dr. Greenwood came in. "You must be Professor Ellen Revere," he said.

"I am," she answered.

Forrester said, "This is Dr. Henry Greenwood with Homeland Security."

Prof. Revere smiled and said, "So you must be the one I get to thank for my wake up call and taxi ride to California?"

Greenwood appreciated her sense of humor and replied, "If you'd like. But now that you're here, what can you tell me about SARV and your experiments on birds and mammals?"

Prof. Revere looked at the small man and asked, "So I can explain it properly, can I get an idea of your background?"

Dr. Greenwood knew she was searching for his credentials and decided to humor her, "I have a doctorate in Biology and Microbiology, I am also an ethologist and I head up the Biotic Crisis Department for Homeland Security and I have extensive field studies of heterotrophs and their ecological impact on other organisms."

Tory asked, "I am sorry, but you said you're an ethio...something? I am unfamiliar as to what that is."

Dr. Greenwood smiled and said, "Ethologist. In other

words, I am an animal behaviorist specializing in communication within and between species."

He continued with a brief explanation to Prof. Revere as he did last night about his extinction concerns and why the government in general, and he specifically, was concerned about the progress, or lack thereof, of their work on preventing this virus from spreading further.

"You know, considering this virus was unknown a couple short months ago, and the lives that have already been saved, I'd say we have done pretty well at holding off a major pandemic to this point," Prof. Revere replied, any humor now gone.

"I am not attacking you," said Dr. Greenwood, "I am just attempting to have all of you see how critically important your work is, and how urgently we need results."

"Sounded a little like an attack to me," said Dr. Forrester.

"It wasn't meant to," explained Dr. Greenwood. "We just need more answers and fewer questions."

"Isn't that always the case?" asked Prof. Revere. "Okay, so let's get back to it. I am going to go organize my lab. As soon as that is done, I can review where we stand with my experiments and what I know today."

As Prof. Revere began to leave, she looked back at Dr. Greenwood and added, "I'll do it quickly."

ʞ ʞ⸓ʞ ʞʞ⸓ʞ ʞʞ⸓ʞ⸓ʞʞ⸓ ʞʞ⸓ʞʞʞ⸓ʞ ʞʞ⸓ʞ

The Northern and Loggerhead Shrikes are called butcherbirds and with good reason. These seemingly innocent looking songbirds have an extremely vicious nature. About the size of a mockingbird, their diet is more like a bird of prey. They are entirely carnivorous, consuming everything from large insects to lizards, rodents, and several other bird species.

Its the way they do it that got them their handle as a butcher. They attack their prey with their hooked beak and either break its neck or whiplash it to death. Once dead, it takes its meal and impales it on a thorn or spike so it can eat at its leisure.

These birds will often kill and impale more than they can eat. These trophies are there to show mates what successful hunters they are and as an overstocked pantry for later meals. They are fearless and will often strike animals more massive than they are, including snakes.

Both of the North American species reside at the Mono Lake Basin in fair numbers.

ᚴ ᚴᛏ ᚴᛏᚴ ᚴᛏ ᚴᛏᚴ ᚴᛏᚴᛏᚴ ᚴᛏ ᚴᛏᚴᛏᚴ ᚴᛏᚴ ᚴᛏᚴ

In Lake Forest, the vultures had found others of their kind in a large tree that housed multiple nests. The other Turkey Vultures had been there for many seasons successfully raising their young. They were tolerant of the newcomers and did not make any threatening gestures when the new birds arrived. With the addition of the two vultures from San Clemente, the tree stood at about a dozen adults.

Although the two vultures were ravenous, they waited until the congregation of birds took wing to help find food with them. They soared ever higher on the warm thermals in search of a smell that would lure them.

Aggressive as the nomadic vultures were, they often associated with others of their kind when they could. Vultures have no vocal organs and are limited to a guttural hiss in communicating their wants and needs. But their movements and actions are sufficient to get their point across to other birds and animals.

As these birds took wing, another flock of birds was on the move in Huntington Beach. To the beach-goers, it had seemed lately every kind of bird harassed them and ruined their peaceful stay by the ocean. Everything from plovers and sandpipers was being uncharacteristically troublesome. They broke into people's possessions pulling out and throwing everything they had brought all over the sand.

Any food was sought after and ruined or consumed by the birds. The gulls and crows were worse, snapping at people as they tried to eat. The birds seemed everywhere. A few people were nearly injured by the birds, and it would only be a matter of time until an accident was reported.

One of the lifeguards was complaining about the bird nuisance and talking to a local policeman reminding him of what took place in San Clemente.

"It certainly is not as bad as there," said the guard. "But the activity has definitely increased, and these birds are getting bolder. I have never known a sandpiper to get near anybody, and now they are grabbing food away from people."

The policeman nodded and said, "I know someone

down in San Juan Capistrano on the force. I heard they had problems down there as well. I think I'll give him a call and see if he knows anything."

He pulled out his phone and looked at his contacts. Seeing the name he wanted, he hit the send button and a moment later said, "Hey John, this is Red Kyle, how are you doin'?"

They exchanged pleasantries for a couple minutes, and then Officer Kyle said. "Listen, John, I want to ask you, we seem to be having a problem with birds around here lately, and I wanted to know what happened in your town and how did the birds act?"

The guard watched Officer Kyle nod, the officer then said, "Really? All over town?" followed by, "No kidding, that bad?"

After several more minutes of conversation between Officer Kyle and the deputy sheriff at the other end, the policemen ended the conversation with, "Well, thanks, John. Yeah, I'll keep you posted. No, seriously, I'll do that. Goodbye, John."

When the call ended, the guard asked, "So? What did he say?"

"It sounds like we might have a bird problem and we may want to get some help for it," said the officer. "Apparently it began in San Clemente kind of like this. As you know, that did not end well. There is a chance our birds might be sick."

An hour later Dr. Forrester's phone rang. When he answered, he heard Dr. Anna Lanz say, "There may be a problem in Huntington Beach with birds. They are becoming aggressive to people on the beach and stealing food."

"Any injuries?" asked Dr. Forrester.

"None reported, yet. The sheriff's department wants to know what they should do?" answered Dr. Lanz.

Start praying, was the thought that popped into Dr. Forrester's mind, but he said instead, "Advise them to start turning people away from the beach is all I can think of, right now."

"That's not much," said Dr. Lanz.

"As Dr. Friedman said to us, we can't be chasing down birds. I would like to get some specimens from there as soon as possible. We need them to test the vaccines. Please talk to her and tell her we need her 'boots on the ground,' as she called them, to get as many as possible."

"She is arranging more people to assist you with the vaccine. She is also working with Dr. Greenwood and others on the way to administer it," said Dr. Lanz. "She and Dr. Abernathy are jammed trying to get you more hands and facilities for your work, here."

"I appreciate that. We may have to put out some type of notice like we did before. We can alert people to the potential for bird attacks and extend it over a wider area," Dr. Forrester said.

"Like Huntington Beach?" asked Dr. Lanz.

"Maybe like California, period," answered Dr. Forrester.

"Are you serious?" she asked.

"If the birds are moving north, as we suspect, they are going to cover a lot of ground. Possibly the entire state and beyond," explained Dr. Forrester. "We can't begin to guess where they have been or how many other birds they may have infected at this point. As Dr. Greenwood said, until we have an antivirus to stop this, it will continue to spread."

ᗱ ᗱᐢᗱ ᗱ ᗱᐢᗱ ᗱ ᗱᐢᗱ ᗱᐢ ᗱ ᗱᐢᗱ ᗱ ᗱᐢᗱ ᗱ ᗱᐢᗱ

At Mono Lake, besides the Peregrine Falcon, there exists the Merlin and Prairie Falcons with their cousins, the American Kestrel. When it comes to birds of prey, Mono Lake has one of the most diverse habitats in the world. There are over fourteen different hawks and eagles, nine types of owls, and more. All the way down to the Turkey Vulture flying around the basin.

It is common to see Bald and Golden Eagles flying about in the same space as a Northern Harrier or Sharp-shinned Hawk. The wide diversity of the biosphere in Mono Lake provides for all types of predators. That along with its relatively close proximity to Yosemite National Park attracts birds from numerous families.

ᗱ ᗱᐢᗱ ᗱ ᗱᐢᗱ ᗱ ᗱᐢᗱ ᗱᐢ ᗱ ᗱᐢᗱ ᗱ ᗱᐢᗱ ᗱ ᗱᐢᗱ

Dr. Friedman and her staff were once again calling in microbiologists, epidemiologists, veterinarians, ecologists, demographers, statisticians, chemists, health economists, health communicators, and information technology experts to all work on the new outbreak. They also communicated to these scientists the dangers, symptoms, and as much information as possible. All the time, helping develop and administer the cure that would finally halt the virus from spreading.

The doctor had set up stations throughout California, Oregon, and Nevada and sent the alert out as Dr. Forrester had suggested to be on the lookout for any suspicious bird activity and to be particularly proactive regarding any strikes from anything with wings, even pet birds, especially if they had not been aggressive previously.

She was now getting the military to get out to places like the landfill and had managed to capture several gulls and crows. They also netted one of the Peregrine Falcons and brought it to the lab.

Several soldiers were out catching birds at Huntington Beach. Here the captures were much more straightforward. They had brought a beach blanket, their nets, and a lot of fresh meat. The birds began flocking to the strips of food almost instantly. Wearing protective gloves, they netted and tagged the birds then placed them in cages at a nearby van and went to collect more.

They caught twenty birds of several species and called to advise the lab they were coming with a full van.

There were three labs set up at UCI, and each one was filled with squawking birds. As rapidly as they could, they drew fluids from each specimen and then immediately vaccinated the birds. Now it was time to see if their vaccine had any effect on the birds.

The biggest problem was they could not test for the rabies virus with a blood test. Prof. Revere found a way to test for the virus using fluids from the birds' nervous system. Similar to a spinal tap in humans but not as invasive. She had shared that information with Dr.

Forrester before they developed the first vaccine.

Unlike a blood test, it took a long time for the results to come in. They had tried to speed up the process, but it was more complicated to analyze the spinal fluid than it was blood. The other drawback was there wasn't a way of performing this test outside a laboratory.

Dr. Greenwood was working with other government departments to find a way to distribute the vaccine once completed. There was one other thing Dr. Greenwood knew that as yet, he did not share with the group. The birds were communicating with each other on a level never seen before.

Upon reading the first report about the "birds of prey" bombardment at the church parking lot, he knew instantly that the birds were planning together, collaborating among the various species, and coordinating in ways that were new to the animal kingdom.

This was further proven by the invasions at the train and the pier. Wherever there were more than one species, there was communication taking place on a scale that did not exist previously. What could not be known was whether this was an enhancement due to SARV, or if this was always possible and the virus just made it more universal.

Dr. Greenwood knew various species had communicated with each other and often helped each other out. Many types of birds act as sentinels warning of hawks and other predators for all kinds of animals. Calling out alarms that alert others to clear and present danger.

Cooperation among different bird species was also usual. Some birds build their nests near larger, more aggressive species to deter predators. Birds like the titmouse and wren will flock with several mixed species to forage for food and to defend territories together. These alliances can continue year after year, indefinitely.

But this went way beyond the norm. These birds were seeking out and collecting other species with a purpose. Dr. Greenwood didn't believe they were trying to infect other birds to kill them but to cooperate and coordinate what they could not do on their own.

The birds were becoming smarter. They were producing military strategies and adding to their numbers like mercenaries in an all-out war. They knew their strength in numbers not only provided more food, which they constantly sought, but also helped them gain dominance over other mammals. They were no longer afraid of man, or anything else for that matter.

The reasons he kept this part quiet were several. He knew that Dr. Forrester and the rest already might be suspecting that the birds were communicating, and did not wish to overstate the obvious to them. But he also did not want to alarm them about how species that never worked together were now coordinating dangerous new tactics.

He needed them to concentrate solely on cures and not exacerbate the issue by adding new behaviors to animals they had studied for years.

The other reason was more personal to Dr. Greenwood. Whenever his specialty was brought to the open, the reaction was always the same. He was taunted about talking to the animals and was dubbed "Dr. Doolittle" and not taken seriously.

It seemed there were times Dr. Greenwood could communicate with other species easier than he could his own. While he thought he might receive more respect from this group, he decided he would test that theory only when it became necessary.

This communication problem, however, concerned him almost as much as the virus, itself. How does one prevent animals from sharing information and diseases with one another? Especially when it is being done on purpose.

Chapter Six

The California Gulls were moving toward the more mountainous terrain north of Santa Barbara into the San Rafael Wilderness area. This area is located in the Las Padres National Forest and was east of the Vandenberg Air Force Base just north of Lompoc.

Several other species had joined the flock. In addition to other seabirds like the Herring Gull and Black Tern, there were several phalaropes and sandpipers, Sooty Shearwaters, and a few ravens. They were moving more northeast and heading along the Interstate 5 freeway. They were looking for food that they could share to quell their hunger. As they were passing over a forest near the Sisquoc River, one of the gulls saw an opportunity it could not resist.

There in a tall but dead Coast Live Oak tree was a huge nest. The gull could see two chicks sitting in the nest all alone. It circled as the other birds continued on. It was too big a temptation for the gull to pass up.

The gull landed on the edge of the nest and eyed the two helpless chicks before it. As it moved closer, it was ambushed by the father eagle who grabbed the gull with its razor-sharp talons. The bird was ripped apart and fed to the chicks before it could realize its end had come. The eagle which often went long distances in search of other food could scarcely believe its luck. This meal came to him, and it was large enough in size to feed not only

the chicks, but both parents, and a yearling which still
hung around the huge nest hoping for an occasional
hand-out.

The other birds continued on their search for
something more substantial that the group could share.
This area was also the home of the Sisquoc Condor
Sanctuary. The giant California Condor with its eight to
ten-foot wingspan is a rare and impressive bird. And this
was its principle protected territory.

These birds were not searching for the condors, but if
this area could keep a giant of that magnitude satisfied,
surely there must be something that could feed a group
like theirs. Especially as they now numbered nearly forty
birds in total.

ᴋ ᴋᵗ ᴋ ᴋ ᴋᵗ ᴋ ᴋ ᴋᵗ ᴋ ᴋᵗ ᴋ ᴋᵗ ᴋ ᴋ ᴋᵗ ᴋ ᴋ ᴋᵗ ᴋ

Things were taking place all over the Southland, as
they refer to it in Southern California. From Laguna
Beach through Irvine, Santa Ana, Garden Grove, parts
of Los Angeles and Santa Monica, Thousand Oaks,
Ventura, and north past Santa Barbara, everywhere
birds were attacking pedestrians, dogs, and anything else
they felt they could successfully take on.

Some assaults were by individual birds, but many
were carried out with several birds banding together.
Most notably gulls and crows, but also shearwaters,
sandpipers, and pigeons joined in the fray. Several people
had numerous scratches and a few with deeper
lacerations. Fortunately, nothing more serious as yet.

All were sent by their doctors to major medical

facilities for rabies shots to stem the virus from taking hold. It was impossible to know which birds were "safe" and which were infected. It was assumed that if a bird actually attacked, it was most likely carrying the SARV. So the medical community treated all patients equally.

At least there had been sufficient time to build up enough doses of the vaccine. The CDC and UCSD continued increasing the antivirus since its discovery after the injuries in San Clemente, not knowing this vaccine was flawed.

San Clemente along with other nearby communities that had been treated with the serum was suffering from a different circumstance. Police were being continuously summoned to homes for complaints of domestic disturbances. A good many of these involved physical abuses toward one or more members of the family.

At first, the responding officers did not connect the two. But upon learning that in almost all of these disturbances, including instances that took place at businesses, the aggressor had been attacked by a bird or birds and received the SARV vaccine. The sheriff's department reached out to the CDC with this new revelation.

Natalie was having another tough day. She was mad at everything and everybody. The day before she gave a terrible time to a grocery cashier over an expired coupon.

"I can't believe you, and this money-grubbing company you work for won't take a lousy sixty cents off this product! Like that would make a difference in the damn CEO's salary," she was heard to say.

Natalie had never complained about anything in her

life or her relationship. She had been a dental hygienist when she met Bill Forrester all those years ago. After graduating from college with degrees in psychology and biology, she became a college professor with her husband at UCSD. As a way to relax, Natalie also was a craftsperson making beautiful pottery and bowls that she sold at local shows when she had time, and gave as gifts to friends and family.

Natalie had always loved her artistry and was proud of her work. Now around the room where she made her creations lie shards of broken pieces that she smashed in anger. She couldn't concentrate, and every time she began a new piece she had to stop to itch her hand where the bird attacked her, swearing a blue streak all the while she scratched at her scar.

Throughout San Clemente and San Juan Capistrano, similar scenarios were taking place. People who couldn't concentrate on their responsibilities in their positions were summoned to their supervisor's office. The worst of these were then fired from their jobs, mostly due to insubordination. It never was a good thing to yell obscenities at your boss.

Like Forresters' strained relationship of late, many families were going through one argument after another over the smallest of reasons. A few couples had separated, with one partner accusing the other of "being a changed" person.

A few relationships sought professional help in the way of counseling or doctors. These lucky few had learned what was causing the angst in their mate or child and were being administered with ointments and prescriptions which helped lessen the problem.

These diagnoses were reported to the CDC, and they began a file and a study of people who were still being affected by their SARV experience.

The CDC, in turn, came to Dr. Forrester and Professor Revere.

It was Dr. Abernathy who brought the bad news, "There is something seriously wrong with the SARV antivirus."

"Come again?" asked Prof. Revere.

"Apparently it has a problematic side-effect. It is causing abnormal aggressive behavior in patients that have been treated with it," Dr. Abernathy answered.

Dr. Forrester had not talked about the uncomfortable conversations he had with his wife, Natalie, as of late. The way they left things when he left for Irvine had not improved in the phone calls he made to her. She was saying horrible things to him, and only one phone call was amiable but still strained.

This new information made perfect sense to Dr. Forrester about what was causing his wife to be so caustic to him after all their years together.

"Damn," was all Dr. Forrester could say.

"Indeed," said Prof. Revere. "Now we have to go back to the drawing board and see if we can determine what is causing the problem before we can proceed further on mass distribution of the vaccine for the birds or people."

Dr. Abernathy said, "Near as we can guess, there must be something that affects the amygdala. Some kind of electrical activation which is causing the aggression."

Dr. Forrester said, "It might also be playing havoc

with the hypothalamus regulating emotion and controlling levels of anger and aggression."

Tory said, "I'm sorry, I am not a med student, which part of the brain are we talking about?"

"The amygdala and hypothalamus are located at the lower rear side just above the spinal cord. They control most of our emotions and fight or flight responses," said Dr. Forrester.

"Whatever it is," said Dr. Abernathy, "we need to fix it and quick. Even if we have to come up with something later to stem these problems that exist in the previous patients."

"Are those patients showing any other side effects other than anger problems?" asked Prof. Revere.

"They complain about constant irritation and itching around the affected area," said Dr. Abernathy.

Dr. Forrester nodded, "Yeah, Natalie is constantly either itching or putting some type of cream or lotion on her hand."

"That's right, she was treated! Has she had any problems with anxiety or anger?" asked Dr. Abernathy.

"Let's just say she hasn't been her normal effervescent self as of late, and leave it at that," answered Dr. Forrester.

Dr. Abernathy shook his head and said, "I'm sorry. I didn't mean to strike a nerve."

"Well, at least I now know it is from the antivirus and not me," said Forrester. "That's some consolation."

Tory spoke up to the trio, "But if the vaccine is working as far as keeping people alive. And presumably would work on the birds, can't we just go with that and solve the other problem later?"

"Not acceptable. If we used the antivirus without addressing this problem, then we might have serious issues going further, and the birds may still continue their attacks," said Dr. Abernathy. "We might just trade one disaster for another. Especially once they have been vaccinated with the incomplete antivirus. We wouldn't be able to determine which birds were attacking from SARV or from the vaccine."

Prof. Revere said, "You are assuming that they would attack after the vaccine. That hasn't been proven."

"No," admitted Abernathy, "But it hasn't been disproved, either. And once administered it could be too late."

"We are running out of time! We can't chuck everything and go forward from square one," said Dr. Forrester.

"We already have labs working on this all over the country," explained Dr. Abernathy. "Dr. Greenwood put the call out even before I came down here. He and Dr. Friedman have been receiving calls from all over Southern California about new bird attacks."

"Why weren't we told?" asked Prof. Revere.

"We were going to let you know when we heard from the sheriff's department about this other predicament," said Dr. Abernathy.

"So we've got a two-fer," said Tory. "I am still not sure why we don't begin vaccinating birds before this spreads to them. As Dr. Forrester said, we are running out of time. If birds are being infected all over California, then we obviously have migrating birds spreading this disease, which was the one thing we had feared all along."

"The birds could still be sick after the vaccine, and we would still be in trouble," Dr. Abernathy patiently explained to Tory.

"Look this isn't the Angry Birds video game," she rebutted, "What happens if we lose millions of birds to SARV? It seems like you are betting the future of the world on the possibility...and that is all it is right now...against a hunch and nothing more."

"And what if we end up losing them anyway from an incomplete antivirus or a vaccine that trades one problem with other issues and still results in death," said Dr. Greenwood who walked through the door as Tory was speaking.

Tory was startled by his voice and jumped.

"Sorry," said Dr. Greenwood, "Didn't mean to spook you, but we still do not yet know if the antivirus works on birds even as well as on people. And if there are side-effects, we don't have time for FDA testing on this. That's why you were given the green light in San Clemente. And thankfully, you did save hundreds of lives. But now we have other issues, and still no guarantee it will work on the birds."

Prof. Revere said to Greenwood, "We are already administering the vaccine on the captured birds that were brought in. Perhaps we can stem the infection if not reverse it completely."

"And how soon will you see the results?" asked Dr. Greenwood, "And I don't just mean the virus but the 'Angry Birds' issue that Miss McKnight mentioned." He smiled at Tory and said, "Angry Birds, I like that."

"We wouldn't know on the second problem," said Dr. Forrester. "Especially as we have no known incubation data on how quickly or severely those effects take place."

"When did you first begin seeing changes in your wife?" asked Dr. Abernathy to Dr. Forrester.

"Aren't we getting a little personal?" Dr. Forrester questioned. It was evident he did not want to air his private problems in front of this group. He had always kept his own individual life separate from his professional career.

Dr. Greenwood approached him and said, "Look, we are not trying to pry. We need a timeline if you can provide it. None of us need details, but if we can determine how long it takes for these, let's call them 'changes,' to begin, we can determine when we could expect it to affect other animals."

Dr. Forrester backed down and said in a low voice, "The itching began within a couple days after her final shot. The moodiness began a day or two after that."

"Can you be more specific?" asked Dr. Greenwood.

Dr. Forrester thought for a moment and said, "I believe it was the morning of the third day. She seemed out of sorts and impatient. It was two days later when I was leaving to come here, and she pitched my luggage at me. She hasn't been right since."

"Wow, under a week," commented Prof. Revere. "Not much time."

"Everything about this virus moves fast," commented Dr. Abernathy. "That's why we lost so many people in San Clemente. And it seems as soon as the SARV comes into contact with a new host, the effects are nearly immediate."

"And now the birds are gaining new recruits on purpose," said Dr. Greenwood.

"I'm sorry?" said Dr. Forrester. "What do you mean on purpose?"

"Dr. Forrester, you were at the pier when the attack came down, isn't that right?" asked Greenwood.

"As was I," said Tory.

"And did you not witness the birds communing and coordinating their onrush together?" questioned Dr. Greenwood to Tory and Dr. Forrester.

"Yes, we had noticed, and Tory saw it two other times with the birds of prey and at the military installation," added Dr. Forrester.

"It was unnerving, to say the least," finished Tory.

"And you didn't figure the birds were trying to work together to increase their numbers?" asked Dr. Greenwood. "You just guessed it was all coincidental?"

"Not entirely," said Dr. Forrester. "But you are suggesting they are deliberately attempting to infect each other. Why? To what end?"

Dr. Greenwood shrugged, "Perhaps they believe they can do more damage and even the odds against other animals. I would guess they do not consider the virus fatal, they only realize they have more cognitive powers and are better able to work together as a group."

"Why wouldn't they have gone beyond San Clemente then?" asked Prof. Revere.

"Perhaps they would have in time. Maybe the flock was coordinating that as well, and your strike at the military grounds ended their plans," said Dr. Greenwood.

"We'll never know for sure, but I would bet this group moving north is attempting to do just that. And so far they are doing a pretty fair job of it."

"What you are suggesting is nothing short of preposterous," said Dr. Forrester.

"I hate to disagree with you, Dr. Forrester," said Tory. "There may be more to Dr. Greenwood's theory then at first look. I saw with my own eyes the multitude of species that were working together at the church and military base. And they were working together, there was no doubt."

"I saw that at the pier, too. It was a coordinated attack, but talking to each other as we are now? That is a little hard to swallow," said Dr. Forrester.

"It didn't happen that way at Bodega Bay," said Prof. Revere. "We know each species struck on their own and no cooperation or coordination was involved. Even with the limited records available, we know that to be true."

"We are convinced now that whatever took place in Bodega Bay was a mutation of the SARV and not the full-blown disease that appeared in San Clemente," said Dr. Greenwood. "The bird or birds that caused the disease there only gave a mild case, so to speak, to the birds in Northern California."

"Which might explain why it never progressed further," said Prof. Revere, nodding her head.

"We have sent your files and samples of your work throughout the country," said Dr. Greenwood getting back to the matter at hand. "You will almost certainly get a lot of questions and calls about the vaccine. I need you three, who are the most familiar with it, to field these questions as quickly as they come in."

"That's not going to leave us much time to do any work, here," said Dr. Forrester.

"I understand, but I would rather you helped hundreds than cowboy this thing on your own. Your lasso isn't big enough," Dr. Greenwood said.

"Okay, we got it, right?" Dr. Forrester asked looking at the other two.

Tory and Prof. Revere nodded and mumbled, "Yeah, we got it."

"Unlike last time, we have days instead of weeks to come up with several solutions and implement them," said Dr. Greenwood. "As they said on the Apollo 13 mission, 'Failure is not an option.' If we don't get this, and in time, most of us won't be here long enough to talk about how we failed. Do what you can here, but make sure others are making progress, and damn quick."

"Good luck," Dr. Greenwood said as he headed out the door.

꙾ ꙾ ꙾ ꙾ ꙾ ꙾ ꙾ ꙾ ꙾ ꙾ ꙾ ꙾ ꙾ ꙾ ꙾ ꙾ ꙾ ꙾

The results were coming back on the captured birds. The initial fluid tests showed that all but two birds showed signs of the SARV pathogen in their fluids. After being inoculated, the results still came back positive for the infectious agent, except in the two unaffected birds.

The healthy birds were also inoculated to prevent the disease from infecting these birds by accident. It seemed like the infected birds were somehow trying to get to the other two.

This meant that the SARV pathogen spread so rapidly, and took hold so wholly, that the infected birds would die from the disease whether they received the vaccination or not, long before their average lifespan. Perhaps a matter of days or weeks, depending on when they became infected.

The birds were making a horrible racket due to their constant need for meat. It was almost impossible to talk above the din, and many times people needed to leave the lab just to clear their heads. It became so bad that ear protection was issued to prevent permanent hearing damage.

Of course, this was in addition to other protective gear they wore to prevent the spread of the virus to those working in the laboratories. They had to set up more lab space so they could review and discuss their findings without the heavy gloves, headgear, and ear protection necessary in the other areas containing the birds.

In one of these external labs, Dr. Greenwood had caught up with Tory and was asking her about the experiences she and Chris witnessed in San Clemente.

"It was beyond frightening, and that was just what we saw firsthand. We had only heard about the boat with the three people that died and the high school students," Tory was saying.

"Actually there were four on the boat," Dr. Greenwood told her, "Seems there was a deckhand with the captain that was also lost and is assumed dead. Those gulls are something. But please, go on."

"Do you know the Latin name for gulls and what it

means, Dr. Greenwood?" Tory asked.

He shook his head.

Tory said, "It's Laridae, it is Greek and means 'ravenous sea bird.' They spend most of their twenty-four-year life span doing nothing but searching for food. You add a wild-card disease like this one in the mix, and you have the brutality of an ocean full of sharks in a blood-soaked environment."

"It's no wonder they picked everything clean down to the bones," said Dr. Greenwood. "And now they are communing with other birds and spreading this epidemic far and wide. I believe down to my soul that the seagulls are our principle culprits behind the expansion of this disease."

"I believe your instincts are correct. Do you know there are over six hundred species of shorebirds alone in California?" asked Tory, "That is just shorebirds and does not include crows, songbirds, pigeons, or birds of prey. And they may be heading to one of the major breeding and feeding grounds as you suspect. There they could spread SARV to millions upon millions of birds throughout hundreds of species."

"Hence the extinction factor that I, and others, are so worried about. Your 'ravenous sea birds' could kill off the world as we know it today," said Dr. Greenwood.

к к┼к к к┼к┼к к┼к┼к к┼ к к┼к┼к к к┼к к к┼к

Throughout the country, every accredited university, sizable medical facility, clinical development, and pharmaceutical company were working on the SARV vaccine. The CDC was coordinating all of these operations from Atlanta and California, and closely following up on the ones having the most success.

They had all received samples of the current SARV antibiotic and were told of the apparent side-effects of the drug. Their orders were clear, make sure the antivirus would halt SARV, eliminate the side effects, and make the drug successful in an airborne form.

The latter was as crucial as the former. It was determined that the only way to administer the vaccine in a fast and capable enough way was to spray the antivirus at a tremendous height and let it filter down to the animals and birds.

This also meant it had to be concentrated enough to prevent the disease from spreading in one dose. So far, two doses minimum were being administered, and three was the recommended dosage. Drs. Friedman, Greenwood, and others knew they would only get one attempt at the birds to prevent further spread or transmission of the virus. After that, with the patterns of migration and movement of the different species, they knew the chances of getting a second dosage to the same birds was slim at best.

Some of the clinics were working around the clock and with good reason. The CDC had guaranteed grant money, or a monetary reward, to the university or company that was the first to develop a workable solution.

The CDC had very deep pockets, but made it a scaleable award that decreased for each day that went without results. Time indeed was money in this race, and big money was at stake.

Dr. Forrester, Prof. Revere, and Tory knew about the outside factors that were taking place in this race for the cure. The same offer held for UCSD and Cornell and they were told to pass it on to their administrators along with the urgency of the situation.

Prof. Revere had already done so upon her arrival and assessment and had a head start at Cornell with every biologist and related field undergraduate working on a solution. Dr. Forrester's campus had also swung into high gear as they wanted to protect their share of the glory for creating the McKnight SARV antivirus, as it was still being called.

Especially since they were now having to field questions from many other campuses and companies working on the cure across the country. There was even speculation that other countries might be involved, particularly with the multi-national firms working on the project.

CHAPTER SEVEN

Less than two thousand years ago, a volcano erupted. When the lava cooled, Negit Island came into being. Over the following centuries, it added to its volume through more eruptions — the last explosion occurring about two hundred years ago. Mono Lake formed two distinct volcanic islands, Negit, and the larger, Paoha Island to the south.

These two islands represent the primary nesting and feeding grounds for the roughly two million birds that flock to Mono Lake. While visitors come to see the fantastic limestone tufa towers that were formed in the lake, and later exposed once the lake was drawn down, most others came to see the birds and wildlife that exist in the area.

The surrounding desert, sagebrush, and extremely high salt content in the lake would surprise most newcomers seeing how many species coexist in the area. Everything from hummingbirds and cuckoos to warblers and plovers occupies the basin. Over 300 various species of birds congregate for the brine shrimp and alkali flies that carpet the floor of Mono Lake.

Most of these birds come to lay eggs and start the process of life and death all over again. Mountain lions and coyotes frequent the area along with mule deer, jackrabbits and gopher snakes. Except for the deer and rabbits, these animals count on eggs and chicks to subsist in this harsh terrain, as do many of the varieties of birds.

Once these birds have brooded their nest and fattened up on the flies, brine shrimp, and sometimes other birds, they fly off to their winter grounds in every direction of the compass. Millions of birds flying all around the world.

Prof. Revere walked into the lab occupied by Dr. Forrester. She walked up to him and announced, "The lab results on the raccoons, dog, and coyote finally came back."

"Oh, and?" questioned Dr. Forrester.

"It's definitely our pet virus," said Prof. Revere.

"So where do you think that leaves us?" asked Dr. Forrester.

"I don't know. We haven't heard anything new from San Clemente. That may or may not mean these were the only animals infected. Or it may mean other animals haven't surfaced in public, yet," answered Prof. Revere.

"I can't believe we were lucky enough for the first scenario. But until we hear something else, it is like the infected birds, we can't go looking for more than we can deal with right here," said Dr. Forrester.

"I think the CDC should put out a warning for potentially dangerous or rabid animals. I think I'll call Dr. Lanz and see if she agrees," suggested Prof. Revere.

"That would be prudent," Dr. Forrester agreed. "By the way, Tory tells me she is now working with you in your lab. Pretty sneaky."

Prof. Revere smiled and said, "Technically she's mine now, anyway. She officially has been accepted at Cornell and her transcripts transferred to us. I was just hoping you wouldn't notice."

Dr. Forrester laughed and said, "Yes, I am so absorbed here. I didn't notice I am missing my right hand. Thanks for letting her point it out to me. So you now owe me one lab assistant."

Prof. Revere was laughing and said as she left, "As soon as I see one standing around the halls, I'll send them directly to you."

Prof. Ellen Revere was feeling good. Not so much about the situation at hand, but more about her station in life. She had never married and lived a solitary life at home. It was the principle reason she was never there.

She enjoyed being with people, but mostly for limited times. Now in her fifties, she thought about how many places she had been. In conversations with Bill Forrester, she knew she had him beat in the number of places on earth she had been to and studied. She also spoke several languages and was able to blend in quite easily in many different cultures, enjoying her travels all the more.

She was as comfortable in Southern California as she was in Ithaca, New York. She was one of the few professors at Cornell without a doctorate, even though she knew more about her field than most. She had her name on as many research documents as any person in her field. It was one of the reasons that she was able to easily lure the shining stars and up-and-comers to Cornell and her program.

Stars like Tory. Prof. Revere knew that she would eventually be one of the top people in ornithology if she stayed with the program. Regardless of what happened with the McKnight vaccine, Tory McKnight was going to go great distances, and Ellen Revere wanted to be the catalyst for her. Prof. Revere had put several students out in the field, and most had done exceptional things already, but she felt Tory could surpass them all.

This is what drove Prof. Revere. She wanted her legacy to be placing people brighter and better than herself in the field. Perhaps they would make the kind of breakthroughs that she had hoped to see in her lifetime. Even though she was far from retirement, and knew there was a great deal more to see and do, she wanted to make sure that there was always someone as eager as herself, or more so, to keep breaking ground once she left the field.

ᴋ ᴌᵗᴌ ᴋ ᴌᵗᴌᴌ ᴋᴌᵗᴌ ᴋᴌᵗ ᴋ ᴌᵗᴌ ᴋ ᴌᵗᴌ ᴋ ᴌᵗᴌ

Complaints were coming into police departments from all over Southern California. Dogs had been injured or killed and eaten; people from senior citizens down to toddlers had been attacked. Many of them beleaguered from multiple birds flocking together, and often of several species. Those with injuries were sent off to already overcrowded medical facilities.

Pigeons to seagulls were dive-bombing pedestrians as they went about their day. Visitors ceased coming to the once popular shorelines and seaside towns. Mayors fumed about their now-deserted beaches and empty stores. People in town were afraid to go outside, particularly after hearing about the warnings of contracting rabies from the onslaught coming from the sky.

The news media was running stories almost nonstop. A gull charged one of the reporters as she did her news report in Long Beach. Her segment went viral throughout the nation immediately. Suddenly reporters were traveling to beaches up and down the coast hoping for a chance for fame serendipitous with that reporter.

Some of the reporters chased the birds hoping to provoke them into charging. The birds mostly flew away or scurried to another part of the beach. After giving up, they tried to find anyone who was attacked or injured. Many of these newscasters ended up at the same overcrowded facilities as the patients, adding to the melee. It got so bad that it was brought under control by the deputy sheriffs called in by the facilities.

Southern California had become the unwilling focus of the nation. Now the same questions that were being asked at UCI and their medical facility were being asked by anchors to supposed experts about the situation before all of America.

The panic began to spread as the doomsayers were pointing to this event as the end of the world. There was a swelling of concern as people in other parts of the nation were searching the skies and calling the police every time a handful of birds landed on a telephone line together.

It didn't end there.

The president and several ambassadors were receiving

phone calls from anxious leaders of other countries. They demanded to know what the U.S. was doing to control this threatening pandemic. These same leaders had consulted with their own country's experts and came to the identical conclusion that it was only a matter of time until infected birds from the United States reached their country.

What began in the quiet seaside town of San Clemente was now a global concern.

The bevy of birds moving north and east toward the I-5 and had crossed into Kern County in California. The birds had found nothing to eat since before they got to the San Rafael Wilderness. Any possible meal they spied moved faster or was protected by the brush and trees of the wilderness.

Now all the birds were rapacious toward anything that moved. They were in full hunting mode and would strike the first animal that came into view. Gotta eat, Gotta Eat!

They flew into the San Joaquin Valley and onto the Elk Hills Oil Field about twenty miles west of Bakersfield.

Two engineers were working on one of the oil pumps performing routine maintenance. They were about to finish up and were gathering their tools and instruments to put back in the truck when they saw them.

The flock circled twice around their heads and then made a beeline directly for the two workers. The birds split into two nearly identical groups and besieged the two men. Ravens and gulls did the worst with their sharp beaks and larger size, but the shearwaters, crows, and the sandpipers also did damage cutting their face, arms, and any exposed areas.

One of the two men made it to the truck, and after fighting off some of the bigger birds, got behind the wheel. He was covered with birds even after managing to get away from his larger attackers. He tried to see his way clear to turn on the ignition but was obstructed by a crow and sandpiper that were pecking at his face. He finally felt the key in the ignition and turned it. He threw the truck in gear just as the crow had rammed home his beak into the engineer's eye.

The man screamed and floored the gas pedal without seeing where he was going. He unintentionally drove the truck into the well pump they had repaired. The truck and pump both exploded in a massive fireball.

The other engineer was laying on the ground far enough from the pump to avoid injury from the blast, but not from the onslaught of birds. After the engineer in the truck had escaped the other birds, the remaining birds flew to the second engineer who was now entirely covered. The birds were unfazed by the thundering explosion, concentrating only on the meal before them.

It wasn't long before the birds had consumed the second man. A few of the birds were lost in the explosion with the truck and the other engineer, but most of them had safely moved to the second victim in time.

Now that they had finally satisfied their hunger and after resting for a while, they flew on toward Mono Lake once more. The gulls knew they needed to avoid the mountains, so they headed east toward Bakersfield. Once past there, they would follow U.S. Highway 395 along the eastern side of the Sierra Nevada Mountains. Otherwise, it would take them extra time to fly up and over the mountain range.

They were now within days of reaching their grounds on Negit Island.

Many of the various breeds of birds had already assembled to Mono Lake. Some of the migrating birds like phalaropes, Caspian Terns, and Snowy Plovers were already nesting with birds who were residents year round. Most birds of prey like the Northern Goshawk, Prairie Falcon, and Golden Eagle never left the area as there was plenty of prey to keep them there all year.

Other birds like the warblers and flycatchers were breeding along the ridges of the basin. The creeks in the watershed contain the highest amount of breeding songbird diversity throughout its thirty-three creeks of the eastern Sierra Nevada Mountains. A few birds, like the local species of Sage Grouse, is highly endangered and not located in any significant number outside Mono Lake.

More and more calls came in demanding test subjects from all the companies and private institutions working on the antivirus. They wanted both infected and non-infected birds so they could test their serums. Dr. Friedman was sending soldiers out to every known community that reported a problem with birds. In that they were fortunate, there was a lot of them.

The bigger issue was how to determine which birds were infected and which were not. There was still no field test they could perform since the virus didn't show up in the blood and drawing the right fluid needed to be carefully extracted in a laboratory setting.

They could not bring all the specimens back to UCI, there wasn't enough room, and there wouldn't be enough time to test each bird there. But that is what was taking place. The two labs overflowed with birds.

Like everyone else at the UCI campus, Dr. Forrester and Prof. Revere were still hoping to provide the solution first. They were the closest to this problem and had the most experience working on it. They had not isolated what caused the "aggression factor" as it was now called, but at least they had an antivirus that prevented death or resulted in physical disabilities.

One pharmaceutical company thought they had resolved the aggression factor, but the animal died a day later, and that antivirus pulled when they determined it was the cause. No one else as yet had come close to improving what already existed.

This was not what anyone wanted to hear.

ᴋ ᴋ ᴛ ᴋ ᴋ ᴋ ᴛ ᴋ ᴋ ᴋ ᴛ ᴋ ᴋ ᴛ ᴋ ᴋ ᴛ ᴋ ᴋ ᴛ ᴋ ᴋ ᴋ ᴛ

Dr. Henry Greenwood was somewhat of an enigma.

Everyone knew by now he was with Homeland Security, but when pressed for a title or department he would say, "I bounce around a lot, and I don't respond well to titles." He would not say any more.

Saying one was with Homeland Security was almost like saying you were an American. This cabinet department of the federal government was the third largest cabinet just after the Department of Defense and Department of Veteran Affairs. Its budget exceeds $40 billion.

Made up of twenty-four different agencies, most citizens have little knowledge of how vast its reach and power is in the country. Anyone who has ever flown knows about the Transportation Security Services or TSA for short, but it is also over agencies like FEMA, Federal Protective Services, Office of Civil Rights and Civil Liberties, and even the Secret Service and Coast Guard, to name but a few.

When someone tries to pin down Dr. Greenwood, he'll most likely say he is in the Science and Technology Directorate, which no one knows enough about to question him further, nor how powerful the lesser-known branch might be.

In truth, Dr. Greenwood is the highest ranking person in Homeland Security not needing Senate approval. He is over many different departments and charged with "fostering interoperability among the Nation's public safety practitioners, so that they may communicate across disciplines and jurisdictions during an emergency." In unofficial circles, they call him "Mr. Fixer."

Dr. Greenwood had always been small. His wife was a

couple of inches taller than him, and she was only five-foot-three. He was picked on and bullied most of his life, often called runt and pip-squeak along with other less than endearing terms. He decided that he would grow up to be more important than them all.

Dr. Greenwood did indeed hold a doctorate in biology along with several other degrees. He decided in high school that he would rather study plants and other animals besides people. However, he got hooked into the political structure and realized that learning to maneuver in those circles successfully would get him a great deal farther than working in the private or educational sectors.

He carefully but successfully moved deeper and deeper into the political structure, all the while advancing without making himself too public. He accomplished every goal given to him by people higher up in the system. This won him their respect and their thanks. He would use the latter to advance to the next higher level.

He carried a tremendous amount of clout, and very few people ever were able to circumnavigate around him without his say-so. Currently, he was involved in several high-level talks with other government officials about the possibility of going with the vaccine they had, instead of waiting until it might be too late.

"The problem is even if we came up with a solution today," he said to the group of thirty people on one phone conference, "we might not be able to make enough of the immunizing agent to distribute to the possible nesting targets to which we think the birds are heading to."

There was a lot of talking concerning this, and one voice came out over the rest. "Dr. Greenwood," the voice fairly shouted, and upon quieting the others, asked, "Do we even know where these infected birds are heading as of yet?"

The voices went silent. Dr. Greenwood answered, "Senator, we believe there are three most likely migration possibilities that these birds are headed. San Francisco, Mono Lake or the Great Salt Lake, with the area of biggest concern being San Francisco. We further believe the infected birds are solely, or primarily, California Gulls."

"I believe the California Gull is revered in Utah if I am not mistaken," said another voice.

"Yes, they have a gilded statue to the bird because it rid the Mormons of grasshoppers and plague. It is at the Salt Lake City Temple Square," answered another.

"I can assure you," said Dr. Greenwood, "If these birds make it to the Great Salt Lake no one will be erecting any statues going forward, because we won't be here. Now, ladies and gentlemen, we need a consensus on how to proceed. We must decide if we will use this vaccine or wait for a new antivirus. This is over my pay-grade to make this decision alone."

The group talked and debated for another hour, arriving at no decision. The discussion went back and forth between distributing the viral cure as it stood and creating a pandemic of a different variety with animals of every species biting and attacking anything that moved. It was finally decided to reconvene after the members had a chance to consult with others in their own circle.

Dr. Greenwood was desperate for a break. Every tick of the clock brought the world closer to an extinction level event not seen since the demise of the dinosaurs. In biology, taxonomy is the science of defining and naming groups of biological organisms by shared characteristics. During his conversations with numerous scientists about the problem facing them, they were in agreement and predicted that if the birds made it to a significant Western Hemispheric Shorebird Reserve Network, or WHSRN, than the world would most assuredly lose 12 percent of its taxonomic families, 75 percent of aviary species and 15 percent of all genera give or take a few percentage points.

A "global catastrophic risk," as they call it in the science community, would ensue. The result would be that one of those taxonomic families facing extinction would be Homo Sapiens. People.

Worse, these predictions stopped at having the birds arriving at the WHSRN and then getting the remaining birds vaccinated. It also took into effect only one WHSRN becoming contaminated. Anything beyond that and the odds against survival were too horrible to contemplate.

Dr. Greenwood tried explaining all that to the group of politicians and leaders but ended up feeling like the man on the sidewalk wearing a sandwich board that said, "The end of the world is nigh!" The others, while realizing the situation was serious, did not seem to grasp the dire consequences before them. Dr. Greenwood heard one member say, "After all, they are just birds."

He knew they were all in trouble.

ᴋ ᴋᵗᴋ ᴋ ᴋᵗᴋ ᴋ ᴋᵗᴋ ᴋᵗ ᴋ ᴋᵗᴋ ᴋ ᴋᵗᴋ ᴋ ᴋᵗᴋ

The local policeman had been cruising back and forth all day long on roads and highways around Santa Ynez and Los Olivos. He handed out a few speeding tickets and had finished having an unusual run-in with a coyote that was being a nuisance at one of the wineries. He dispatched the animal and knew he would have a lengthy report to file for discharging his weapon. He was thinking about this as he headed down the deserted road from the winery back toward Highway 154.

Other than the coyote incident, it was a fairly ordinary day, and he was close to the end of his watch. He was less than a half-mile from the highway when he saw a large injured bald eagle near the side of the road. The officer pulled his vehicle over to the side and a little behind the eagle. He did not want to spook the bird into injuring itself further.

He got out of the car and slowly approached the bird. He had seen eagles flying in and out of the San Rafael Wilderness before but had never gotten this close to one. He saw the eagle had one of its wings extended and the other folded. The officer figured the bird must have been struck by a vehicle and couldn't fly.

As he carefully moved to the bird, it began hopping away from the policeman. The bird hobbled further into the brush. The officer thought he should radio this in and let the National Park Service handle this, as he knew nothing about birds in general, or eagles, specifically. He figured they would want to know how seriously he thought the bird was hurt, so the policeman decided to see if he could ascertain at least that much.

He moved into the brush where the eagle had just gone. He could see the bird about twenty-five yards ahead. It still had its wing out and was hopping away but slower than before. He gained some ground on the bird and was nearly on top of it.

The officer saw a brief shadow and then felt the searing pain of talons piercing his shoulders and neck. He never saw the two adult eagles, since he was concentrating on the injured eagle before him. They attacked once he was in place.

The last thing the trooper saw was the "injured" eagle stand up and begin flapping its wings looking for its opportunity to strike. The two adult eagles drove him face down into the ground. He tried to reach his gun, but the yearling eagle had landed, digging its claws into his arm and back paralyzing the policeman in pain. No man is a match for three starving eagles. The officer was dead moments later.

ᛕ ᛕ ᛕ ᛕ ᛕ ᛕ ᛕ ᛕ ᛕ ᛕ ᛕ ᛕ ᛕ ᛕ ᛕ ᛕ ᛕ ᛕ ᛕ ᛕ

Dr. Greenwood, Dr. Forrester, Prof. Revere, and a room full of biologists were trying to figure where the birds causing the infection to spread might be. And more importantly, they needed to know where the birds were heading. It was bad enough to not have a working antivirus as yet, but they were also working on an aerial antivirus to vaccinate the birds from the air. They needed to know where to start once it was created and tested.

The group tried to make a pattern of the bird invasions starting in San Clemente and moving north. Reports had come from Newport and Huntington Beach, Oxnard, and Ventura, which made sense since they suspected these were shorebirds. But they also had dispatches from more inland towns like Irvine and Thousand Oaks. This further led them to believe it was the gulls, as any other shorebird would stay closer to the ocean's edge. Many gull species traversed the country, and a year-round population exists in all the northwestern states, particularly in Utah and Washington.

The gulls, being so diversified did not help the group narrow down where they were going. They first looked at the critical nesting grounds outside San Francisco. The scientists knew gulls were most abundant in the Alviso, Mowry, and Newark salt ponds, making up tens of thousands of birds. The landfills also contained several thousand gulls using this as a natural food habitat. The most massive dump being the South Bay refuge, with nearly 4,000 California Gulls alone feeding there.

If the gulls made it there, and the unaffected birds had not received the vaccine in time, it could infect dozens of species. The overall size of San Francisco also made the logistics of administering the vaccine quickly enough nearly impossible. First, was the problem that it was so spread out with numerous targets. When the ocean winds and fog were also factored into the equation, the vaccine scarcely had a chance to do what it was hoped it would to do.

The next largest area would be the Great Salt Lake, which actually contained the most birds. Over ten million birds and two-hundred-sixty species stop there throughout the year. The American White Pelican existed in the millions here, but pelicans were immune to SARV. The current antivirus had been created from the Brown Pelican.

Because the Great Salt Lake is mostly a migratory area, the birds stay long enough to breed and add weight for their long journeys and then move on to other parts of the world. This area would present the greatest threat, with the disease attaining global distribution and affecting the highest number of traveling birds at once.

The third most urgent area was Mono Lake. It was a smaller but heavily concentrated area containing three hundred species of all types living or visiting the area. While many were resident songbirds, waterfowl, and birds of prey, Mono Lake had the most massive migration of grebes, gulls, American Avocets, and Black-necked Stilts, to name but a few. Two million birds compacted into this relatively small area throughout the summer and fall seasons, compared to the other two habitats.

This area was the greatest substantial threat because of the number of species it contained and the diversity of the areas those species traveled around the globe. On the plus side, Mono Lake would be the easiest to vaccinate from the air because of its compact size.

In Lake Forest, several birds from starlings to gulls had joined up with the vultures. A Great Horned Owl also began hunting with the group. Since the vultures were not birds of prey, primarily because their talons were too soft to catch other animals, the addition of different varieties of birds made finding and grabbing food easier.

As a result, the swarm caught numerous smaller animals, thanks in large part to the owl, and even managed a couple of cats and a little dog. As the size of the group increased, so did their daring. The gulls and crows now fiercely charged people and bigger dogs. They had inflicted numerous injuries, but no kills.

The birds increased their range as well, flying into neighboring towns like Irvine and Mission Viejo. They needed more "fire-power" and were recruiting new birds in each new area to their dangerous flock.

What began with a dozen vultures now numbered forty-seven birds.

CHAPTER EIGHT

Armed security guards now were assisting workers at the Bowerman landfill. They were there to keep the birds from striking workers and those drivers bringing trash to the fill sight. They were hired shortly after the worker had been murdered at the center of the dump. They had orders to shoot any birds that looked threatening. They had built a pretty good pile of dead birds.

Also at the facility, a new operation was set up by the military. They were under orders to trap and remove as many of the infected birds as they could safely get. There were countless laboratories needing the specimens, unhurt if possible.

The lieutenant in charge of the operation had posted soldiers at all four points of the compass with the same specialized mortars that were used at Steed Park in San Clemente. The soldiers had begun operations early that morning to attract as little attention to themselves as possible.

After a couple hours of lying low, a truck pulled into the center of the area, and three soldiers got out and went to the rear. They opened the back and pulled out an entire side of beef, placing it equidistant of the mortar positions.

They hurried back into the truck and pulled away. The men stationed at the mortars did not have long to wait. The soldiers watched as a few gulls came to investigate. The soldiers held their position and did not move a muscle. The birds flew off without touching the beef.

Ten minutes later they saw the swarm forming in the air above them. There were hundreds of birds from crows all the way down to mockingbirds. All flew together in a tight circle. A minute or two later the birds could not resist the feast below them and landed on the remains of the cow. They began tearing at the meat as if they hadn't eaten in a week or more.

All four mortars fired simultaneously trapping the birds under the four nets. Because of the smaller size birds, they needed to use all the nets to make it impossible for anything to escape, which none did. The birds were squawking furiously under the nets with the din making it difficult for the soldiers to hear their orders over the racket.

The truck returned and opened the back again revealing dozens of cages, Using protective gloves a dozen soldiers including the lieutenant, carefully pulled the birds out from under the nets and placed them in the cages.

The operation took almost ninety minutes to secure all the birds. A couple of birds nearly got free, but another soldier would suddenly appear to keep the bird contained. They had to put several birds into each cage to carry them all, and even then, almost did not have enough containers. They had underestimated the number of birds that would come to feed.

The soldiers accomplished the first part of their

mission. To capture infected birds and bring them to the waiting labs at UCI. The second part of their orders was trickier, as they now had to collect birds that seemed unaffected by the virus. They still had not come up with a plan for that order.

Dr. Forrester spoke softly to Natalie on his call the evening before. Now that he knew what was causing her angst toward him, he realized he was talking to a different person than his wife of almost twenty years.

Natalie was still agitated and cursed every other sentence, something else Forrester was not accustomed to from her. He tried asking about her day, and she said, "I can't get a fucking thing done around here because of this constant damn itching. I am ready to cut my fucking hand off to get rid of it."

"Somehow, my dear, I don't think that would solve your problem, or be very prudent," Dr. Forrester said to the stranger on the other end.

"What the hell would you know about it?" Natalie lashed out. "You're all nice and cozy with your goddamned girlfriends up there, while I am totally miserable down here. Do you even give a shit? I think not!"

The conversation continued for a little longer with Dr. Forrester trying to soothe his wife while she spat venom from the other end. When he hung up a tear escaped his eye from the frustration and hurt he felt for his wife and what she was going through.

He had tried to suggest that she see their physician for something to help her get through her day. She would hear none of it, taking offense that he thought there was something wrong with her. All of this peppered with a string of curses toward him.

Most ornithologists work for land and wildlife agencies at the federal and state levels or nonprofit conservation organizations. Some work at zoos, wildlife parks, and as veterinarians and environmental scientists, though these jobs are far less exclusive to birds. But Bill Forrester felt his urge to teach and conduct research at a university. As it turned out, that became his entire life especially once he met Natalie.

Dr. Forrester met his wife while she was going to college. He was an adjunct professor in biology working part-time at the university, while also studying for his doctorate. Natalie was working in her post-graduate studies in psychology.

They met at the student union and became fast friends. They did their best to see each other, but between his teaching and studying, they were barely able to spend more than an hour or two together every couple weeks. However, they enjoyed each other's company so much that they rode it out for two years. They both received their advanced degrees in the same summer. Forrester received his doctorate in Zoology along with a masters degree in Environmental Toxicology.

That second degree was what Dr. Forrester was utilizing the most for the current situation with the birds. Environmental toxicology is the study of how toxic chemicals affect organisms and the environment. It determines how the chemicals move through ecosystems, how they are absorbed and metabolized by the animal, the mechanisms by which they cause disease, and how those effects may be treated, minimized, or reversed.

Dr. Forrester married Natalie that September and they both began teaching at the university where they graduated. Because he needed research and studies to continue his teaching credentials, he and Natalie traveled around the world studying different species and migration patterns every summer. Natalie enjoyed the exotic locations they visited. She always said she was happy to help her husband in his field research claiming it was a nice distraction from dealing with the problems of people.

Natalie became pregnant in their third year together and had their one and only child in April the following year. Their son, Riley, was now seventeen and a foreign exchange student in Spain. He was currently spending the summer there.

Under the present circumstances, Dr. Forrester thought he would be eternally grateful for this. Even though it left Natalie by herself, he guessed that an over-exuberant teenager would be the worst problem Natalie would be able to face currently.

Natalie complained during every call about dealing with her students and their litany of excuses and problems about completing assignments. She had a light summer schedule but still said how sick and tired she was of them and wanted to leave the school and its headaches behind for good.

Her husband again knew this was the complications

from the vaccine talking. Natalie had always loved her students and her chosen profession. Even though she was a psychologist herself, Dr. Forrester knew why she was unable to figure out that she was not in control of her normal feelings. The problem was the side-effect of the vaccine. She was unable to reason her emotions out while under the side-effect from the drug's influence. He secretly prayed that his wife would hold together for a little while more.

Dr. Forrester knew he should be with his wife. Even if only to get her to their doctor. He could assist her in coping with her malady until a genuine solution was found. He decided to contact a couple other people in her department to help keep an eye on her and assist getting through her day. After explaining Natalie's problem, he could hear an audible relief from them as they had noticed her changes and did not know the cause. They agreed to do what they could.

The entire situation made it hard for Dr. Forrester to focus on what he was doing. He continually wondered what Natalie might be doing or saying to others in his absence. Something he was never concerned about before.

Dr. Forrester received some hope and good news concerning his wife's condition the next morning. One of his medical colleagues at UCSD thought he might have isolated the problem. He had been working with several other doctors in San Clemente on people who had been affected by the rabies vaccine.

Many of the patients that were acting violently were being treated with drugs to help calm them down. They learned that the more combative the person was before the rabies vaccine treatment, the worse the symptoms became.

Those that already had terrible tempers or were prone to violence and lashing out, had to be contained and even strapped to the bed to prevent injuring others, particularly the medical staff.

After numerous tests and scans they were able to determine that after the patient received the treatments for rabies, an enlarging occurred of one of the two almond-shaped amygdalae at the base of the brain just above the spinal cord. This resulted in hyperactivity of the amygdala.

Whenever a patient has one amygdala that is smaller than the other, it resulted in fear and anxiety disorders. Fear feeds the emotional response to danger, whereas anxiety is a psychological response which causes the patient to perceive they are in danger.

Anxiety disorders that are associated with the amygdala include Obsessive Compulsive Disorder (OCD), Post-Traumatic Stress Disorder (PTSD), Borderline Personality Disorder (BPD), and social anxiety disorder.

Apparently, the last of these, the social anxiety disorder was the result of being overstimulated and causing the patient to lash out physically and psychologically toward others. The person affected became irrational and hostile. They needed to treat this enlarged part of the brain to bring control back to the patient.

Why the rabies virus had affected this gland was still a mystery, but at least they had a place to begin. It may have had something to do with the pelicans they derived the vaccine from. They already knew that birds had a much faster metabolism than humans. This was the primary reason they thought the virus acted so fast and spread so quickly.

But to cause a swelling of one of the two amygdalae made little sense. Why not affect both? And does that also cause a problem with the hypothalamus that it is attached to? The hypothalamus acts as a regulator of emotion controlling levels of aggression and anger.

Figuring out how to bring these regulators back under control, or prevent this reaction in the first place, was anything but a surety. Doctors had been trying to regulate these problems in patients and return them to more normal behavior for years without a long-term solution.

They had achieved some success with a combination of drugs, but the enlarged amygdala hadn't reduced to its usual size as yet. They at least now knew the problem and were working toward a cure.

Dr. Forrester wondered about inviting Natalie up to visit his colleague at San Clemente. He was concerned about her driving all that way in her current emotional state. He also guessed that after his suggestion from last night's call, her reaction to his idea would be met with anything less than enthusiasm.

Then again, he would risk almost anything for a chance to talk to his real Natalie again.

As Dr. Forrester was contemplating all this, the soldiers arrived with the captured birds. They began unloading the cages and stacking them in the hallways by the labs that he and Prof. Revere were occupying. He stopped the lieutenant and tried to convince the officer that they had no room or facilities to take care of all the additional birds he was bringing.

"Sorry, sir," the soldier said, "That's my orders. I am to get these to you as quickly as possible. Then I am to go round up some more. What you do with them after that is not in my purview."

The lieutenant then headed back to the truck for more cages.

Prof. Revere came out of the lab and put her hand to her mouth to stifle a laugh, shaking her head.

Tory came out of the lab and said above the squawking, "What the hell?"

Prof. Revere lost her control at that point, she began laughing out loud and returned to her already noisy and overcrowded laboratory.

Dr. Forrester shrugged and said to Tory, "We are going to have to find a home for these and be careful, I believe these birds are infected."

Because of all the noise in the labs and halls that the birds made, a quiet office was loaned to the people working in the wing and away from the cacophony. Forrester had spent a good deal of time there lately talking to other companies and universities about the SARV situation.

He went there now to make calls to all those places that were demanding samples of birds on which to experiment on. He had them, and by God, they were welcome to them.

The migrating gulls had made it past Bakersfield and were now into the hilly terrain north of Tehachapi. While the hills were steep, going this direction allowed them to end up on the east side of the Sierra Nevada Mountain range.

Instead of trying to fly over mountains that were ten to fourteen thousand feet high they could follow along the Los Angeles Viaduct that brought precious water from the north to the south. Between the viaduct and U.S. Highway 395, they knew they would come across food on their journey.

But they were not quite there yet. The incident at the oil reserve had slowed the birds down. And the full meal they had there took its toll as well. The birds were moving slower than they ever had, but they were making progress. The weather was working with them, and they were seeing landmarks that most of them had seen for several years.

They were almost back.

Drs. Friedman and Abernathy burst into Dr. Greenwood's office. Dr. Friedman said, "We may have gotten a good ping as to where the birds are headed."

Dr. Greenwood looked up and said, "Tell me."

"There was a policeman killed near Los Olivos," said Dr. Abernathy. "We sent someone over there to verify this, but we are pretty sure it was birds based on the description of the body."

"Where is Los Olivos?" asked Greenwood.

"It is a little east of Lompoc and Vandenberg, but fairly close to the coast," answered Dr. Friedman.

"Well, what're your thoughts?" asked Dr. Greenwood.

"We think the target is San Francisco," said Dr. Friedman. "The birds are staying west and hugging the coast. That would rule out the Great Salt Lake completely, and it doesn't seem like Mono Lake would be a candidate as they should be heading further east by now."

Looking at a map on his desk of California, Dr. Greenwood said, "It also puts them further south than where we guessed they'd be by now. That could buy us an extra day, maybe even two."

"We could use it," commented Dr. Friedman.

"Yeah, but San Francisco, damn," retorted Dr. Greenwood.

"The worst of the three scenarios," said Dr. Friedman, nodding her head in agreement. "Not in population but definitely in the amount of area to be covered."

"I was pulling for Mono Lake, myself," said Dr. Abernathy.

"What makes you so sure it's our birds and not a random group?" asked Dr. Greenwood.

"This is the furthest north of any incident we have heard. Also, the isolated nature of Los Olivos leads us to believe it's got to be our flock. There is nothing but a few wineries around that location," said Dr. Abernathy.

"At least we have a possible target now," said Dr. Greenwood. "Let me know the moment you get confirmation that it was a bird incident from Los Olivos. I will give the word for the airplanes, equipment, and men I have standing by to be moved into place. We could be ready within hours of a decision. How are we doing on a workable vaccine?"

For the next twenty minutes, Dr. Friedman gave a rundown on the various firms and schools that seemed closest to finding a cure. Cornell and UCSD were still in the running, but more toward the middle of the pack.

None were close enough to suit Dr. Greenwood. "Damn, I was hoping we'd be closer. What else can we do to push these people?"

Dr. Abernathy said, "Many are working twenty-four-seven already. Especially the big firms and schools. We have already offered that huge reward..."

"Please, Dr. Abernathy. It is a grant, not reward, just like your name...Grant," Greenwood smiled at the man.

"Okay," Dr. Abernathy corrected himself, "Grant. Anyway, that along with the exclusive patent we are offering them is every motivation we can come up with for this."

"Maybe fame? Nobel Peace Prize, Man or Woman of the year on Time, something like that?" asked Dr. Greenwood.

"We could drop hints about that, but I think the money angle is still our biggest hook," said Dr. Friedman, "Besides, I am not sure throwing more into the pot will make this machine move any faster right now. They have been made extremely aware of what is at stake."

"Yes," agreed Dr. Abernathy, "If we fail there may not be another Peace Prize or much of anything going forward."

Dr. Greenwood nodded his head, and then his phone rang. The other two doctors excused themselves.

"Greenwood," he answered. "Uh huh, okay let's hear it." He tapped his desk to get the attention of the two doctors and waved them back in."

When they returned to their seats, Greenwood said, "Wait a moment, I have two doctors with the CDC here with me, and I want them to hear this and ask you any questions they may have." Then to the doctors he said, "I have Dr. Sam Hoskins on the line from Cornell." He put the phone on speaker mode.

"Yes, well, as I was saying, we isolated the problem with the aggression factor in the antivirus. It seems the pelican DNA that was used increased the amygdala which affected the hypothalamus, causing an electrical 'short-circuit' in the patient and triggering an anxiety and anger response." the voice at the other end said.

"Have you been able to reverse the process?" asked Dr. Friedman.

"Yes, and no. We were able to cancel out the reaction from the gene that caused the side-effect, and we are reasonably sure we now have a working antivirus without the aggression factor," said the voice. "However we have not devised a cure for those previously treated, yet."

"How reasonable on the antivirus?" asked Dr.

Greenwood.

"Ninety-eight percent. As soon as we get back a couple more tests, it will probably be ninety-nine or better," answered the voice.

"Since you are with Cornell, do you know, or work with, Professor Ellen Revere?" asked Dr. Greenwood.

"She's the one that told me to call you, immediately," answered Dr. Hoskins. "She said it couldn't wait for her to get over to your office."

There was a knock on the door, and an out-of-breath Prof. Revere stuck her head in, beaming with pride. Dr. Greenwood enthusiastically waved her in and gave her the thumbs-up sign with his hand. For the first time since getting together, all the occupants were smiling.

After the call ended, Dr. Friedman looked at Dr. Greenwood with a smirk and said, "I guess you got your wish. We have a workable vaccine."

$$\kappa\,\kappa^\dagger\kappa\ \ \kappa\,\kappa^\dagger\kappa\ \ \kappa\,\kappa^\dagger\kappa\ \ \kappa\,\kappa^\dagger\ \ \kappa\,\kappa^\dagger\kappa\ \kappa\,\kappa^\dagger\kappa\ \ \kappa\,\kappa^\dagger\kappa$$

Prof. Revere had told neither Tory nor Dr. Forrester about the phone call from Dr. Hoskins, for three reasons. First, while they were able to isolate the offending gene in the antivirus, they had not found a cure for those who had been treated previously. That meant there still wasn't a cure for Natalie Forrester, yet. She did not wish to disappoint Dr. Forrester with that news.

Secondly, the final results had not come in yet, and she did not want to announce the new vaccine prematurely. If something went wrong she didn't wish to celebrate before there was a genuine reason.

The other reason was if the cure actually worked as Hoskins said, it meant that Cornell, and not UCSD, would be in line for a significant windfall from the U.S. Government, which would be a painful blow to Forrester, personally and professionally. She knew he would have to find out, but wasn't sure how to tell him.

She did ask the other three in the room she had left at the CDC to keep this quiet, at least until the final results came in. Then she would share the news with the others. But the CDC was already proceeding as the antivirus was a done deal, at least regarding it as cure to SARV.

Finally, there was still a speed-bump in all this. Dr. Hoskins explained to Dr. Greenwood and the others that while they may now have the vaccine, they did not yet have an aerosol version of the cure. So far, the aerosol tests on uninfected birds and mammals had not provided the results they hoped. When the test subjects were sprayed, and then later infected, it resulted in the animals being more resilient to the virus, but it still showed up in their fluids. This was unlike when they inoculated an individual bird or mammal using a syringe.

The good news on the spray version was the disease did not manifest itself as it did before. The tremendous hunger and the aggressiveness did not show up in the newly infected subjects. Nonetheless, the virus still existed. There was the possibility that it might end up killing the animal anyway, and the infected animal might again spread SARV in this form to new victims. They would not know the first part for weeks or longer.

They were about to test the second part that day. At

least they were working on the aerosol part of the equation with a better solution then they had before. However, they did not know if the animal infected a new specimen, whether the original strain of SARV would return or if the current lessened strain would appear.

The doctors and professors of Cornell were close to the final answer, and they felt it. They promised everyone that their laboratories were burning the lights around the clock. Too much depended on it.

ᴋ ᴋᵗᵗ ᴋ ᴋᵗᵗ ᴋ ᴋᵗᵗ ᴋ ᴋᵗ ᴋ ᴋᵗᵗ ᴋ ᴋᵗᵗ ᴋ ᴋᵗᵗ

The mission commander for the aerosol spraying was Air Force Lieutenant Colonel Mark Washburn. He was in charge of the hundred plus Reserve Citizen Airmen, based at Youngstown Air Reserve Station, Ohio, all currently working from a base of operations at the Travis Air Force Base near San Francisco.

Lt. Col. Washburn added to this group the 502nd Operations Support Squadron, based at the Kelly Field Annex, and the 433rd Maintenance Group, from Lackland Air Force Base. All were in ready and waiting for the aerosol and their first destination. On the tarmac sat four C-130H Hercules aircraft with the Aerial spraying 2 MAFF units. An Air Force Reserve Modular Aerial Spray System, or MASS, was attached to each of the cargo decks of aircraft.

The C-130H spray aircraft currently at the base at Travis were all delivered in the late 1980s and early 1990s. Assigned to Air Force Reserve Command's 910th Airlift Wing, the 757th AS is the only large-area, fixed-wing aerial spray unit in the US Department of Defense.

These specialized aircraft featured upgraded electrical connections, paratroop doors with a sealable port that accommodated four-inch diameter pipes for the spray nozzles, and internal plumbing for an inner and outer sets of spray bars mounted under each wing. The outer spray bars on the wings were not being used for this mission, as it was more important to give a greater concentration of the spray to each area instead of applying the vaccine over too wide a surface. This minimized the amount of pathogen needed to cover all the animals below. The nozzles and spray bars were installed on the aircraft after their arrival at Travis from their base in Ohio, to minimize the chance of damage to them.Each plane could carry a maximum of one thousand gallons of vaccine. The four aircraft he currently had were the only ones of their kind set up for the spraying of dispersants like the vaccine.

This same system had been employed in San Antonio, Texas, for the recovery efforts against mosquitoes after Hurricane Harvey in 2017. There they sprayed more than 1.4 million acres of insecticide to control the bugs nesting in the polluted waters of the area. They also did the spraying after Hurricanes Katrina and Rita in 2005, and Hurricane Gustav in 2008, treating nearly three million acres total.

All they needed now was the agent to spray and their flight orders.

Dr. Greenwood had a new dilemma on his hands. Should he advise the "powers that be" that a new vaccine that worked had been manufactured, but not the aerosol equivalent? Would they demand Dr. Greenwood begin administering it, even knowing that it wasn't complete? He knew these politicians and the quickest answer was always the best for them. Screw the consequences.

Or does he stay quiet for the moment and pray that Cornell adjusts the vaccine enough to get it to work in aerosol form? If he waited, would he be condemning the world faster than the politicians? And how long would it take to produce enough of the aerosol version when it was created to cover San Francisco? Dr. Greenwood was already pushing the limits of his authority in all this. He wondered if he dare make a decision of this magnitude on his own.

One thing he knew absolutely, there would be no second prize if he guessed wrong, or if he let others make a bad call. Dr. Greenwood guessed that he had at most a week until the gulls reached the bays and landfills of San Francisco. Possibly less. And naturally, the birds would continue to infect others along their route as they had been doing. Some of those newly-infected birds might also migrate to other areas. There was no way to know.

Even today, if he put every lab and medical facility on the job of creating the antiserum to the virus, they may not have enough to blanket the vast San Francisco Bay area in time, let alone all the other possible locations.

Another problem was, if the virus could be spread and ended up killing the birds in mass, the same end

game would result. Of course, if Greenwood used the
current new vaccine and the sprayed animals did not
cause the virus to spread, they might have enough time
to refine the vaccine into a final answer.

Delaying his decision might be the death of them all.

Dr. Greenwood thought about his wife and two little
girls at home in Washington, D.C., Whatever his
decision, it would inevitably affect them like the rest of
the world. He pulled a bottle of scotch out of his lower
drawer and poured some into his coffee cup.

God, grant me clarity, he thought and leaned back in
his chair contemplating the labyrinth of possibilities
before him.

When the supervisor of the men at the Elk Hills
refinery finally discovered his missing engineers, he
immediately called the police and reported the terrible
accident at the pump.

Two squad cars arrived, and three policemen and a
policewoman exited the vehicles. Three of the officers
went over to the second engineer lying on the ground and
stared in disbelief at the remains.

"God almighty," said a younger officer. "What do you
think happened to him?"

The policewoman looked at the body and the distance
from the pump, "My guess is he was seriously injured
from the explosion, crawled over here and died, and then
a coyote or two got to him."

"How did he get away from the blast to way over

here?" asked an older officer, "And where is the blood trail from where he sustained his injuries?"

"So what do you think happened?" asked the supervisor.

"I really couldn't say," answered the officer. "I can't imagine what could tear up a body like that. Not even coyotes work that fast or completely. And I also can't figure what would cause your man to drive his truck into that pump over there. Something is awash, here. Big time."

The fourth officer was by the burned-out truck and pump. He looked at the charred remains of the driver, but then saw something else. There were the blackened, burned-out bodies of three birds.

"Hey," he called to the others, "What do you make of this?"

$$K K^K K K K^K K K K^K K^K K K^K K K^K K K^K$$

At Dr. Greenwood's suggestion, FEMA had been called in after the governor of California declared a state of emergency. They needed additional assistance because of the growing number of bird attacks in the Southland. The new virus was already being dispensed for people that had been newly injured by birds.

FEMA was trying to get the injectable vaccine into as many medical centers as possible. This had become an urgent matter, not just from the number of persons being wounded by birds, but because they did not want medical centers using the antivirus containing the aggression factor in it. That vaccine would only exacerbate the problem, and the patients would need to return to be retreated for that side-effect when a cure for that problem was finally discovered.

A bigger issue was SARV was spreading through more birds every day. Communities that had been previously unaffected by aggressive birds were beginning to see the birds' habits change before their eyes. Towns from Rancho Santa Margarita down to Dana Point were monitoring changes in the bird species, as warned by the CDC and the sheriff's office.

The birds began flocking more often with several different types flying around together. They also were flying closer and closer to people that were walking around by themselves. It was as if they were testing the vulnerability or danger threat in each individual. A couple of assaults took place in these newly concerned cities but without injury, thus far.

People were being warned not to go out alone if at all possible. Many new products were appearing in stores to help ward off the winged aggressors like the "Bird Basher," which was nothing more than a re-branded mini-baseball bat like they sell at stadiums, or "Bird-B-Gone," an umbrella-type heavy mesh screen that would open up and supposedly protect the user from birds getting too close.

Residents became more panic-stricken and were requesting the vaccine before they could be hurt from a rabid bird. Those people were turned away. There was scarcely enough antivirus around to treat the already injured people. Doctor's offices, urgent care facilities, and medical centers had to be sparing with what they had, and most smaller offices had none at all.

A waiting list of people needing the new vaccine was forming, and it was getting longer by the hour. Many patients from the smaller doctor's offices were referred to more extensive medical facilities that had the new vaccine. These doctors knew that time was critical in treating the SAR virus.

Dr. Friedman had done everything she could to make sure that the production of the vaccine would keep up with demand as closely as possible. She had set up abandon warehouses around the country as labs to reproduce it. It was difficult establishing clean rooms and the stringent sanitary conditions for these old and deserted buildings. She had national guard troops from each state where they were located helping to clear the warehouses out and set up the necessary equipment.

Many companies participated in creating the vaccine and were charging handsomely for their efforts. Insurance companies in California were having to foot part of the bill, but the majority was being handled under a federal emergency proclamation in the interest of public safety.

Dr. Friedman was still about twenty percent short of the current demand, but she hoped they would catch up shortly. She also knew as soon as they had a working aerosol of the vaccine, she would have to switch almost everything over into making that version. Dr. Greenwood had others working in Homeland Security seeking additional possible manufacturing facilities. Dr. Friedman knew she would soon need them.

While a couple labs were working on a cure to the

aggression factor, the majority were putting all their efforts into creating the new SARV vaccine. Doctors were left to treat the hundreds of patients that survived the first wave of attacks with whatever medications they could to minimize the patient's anger and depression issues.

Infected birds were flying all over the country, but not under their own power. These birds were being transported by cargo planes to various cities to be distributed to those working on developing a cure for SARV. One such shipment was sent to the Cornell Lab of Ornithology in Ithaca, New York.

They needed both infected and healthy birds to continue their experiments. The infected birds were showing up regularly now, but the healthy birds were harder to attain. All of the pet shops around the country had been wiped out of inventory. The cockatoos disappeared first, as this was the species that first carried the virus. Other types of parrots, like macaws and gray parrots, followed. Lastly, the smaller birds of any kind were sold.

There was a growing black market developing for birds, especially of the parrot species, to the point where some pet birds had suddenly gone missing from their homes. Others birds were being offered up for sale by their owners due to the fear factor about the rabies virus endlessly appearing on the news and social media.

People began selling their carrier pigeons at

outrageous prices. Other civilians had taken to trying to catch birds, especially pigeons and crows for the growing bounty that had been offered by companies for them. A few of the labs tried using chickens and turkeys, but the birds died the very next day. Waterfowl was being tested and with better, or at least longer lasting, results. Something in the makeup of the chickens and turkeys reacted severely to the virus the moment they were injected. The word went out quickly not to use them.

The military was still trying to catch wild, healthy birds, but with limited success. Their orders had changed from needing the infected birds to needing only uninfected fowl. Even using the nets that they employed in the capture of diseased birds did not work well. The healthy birds were not flocking as the infected aviary did. Also, there wasn't a bait that would attract the birds in any significant number. The few birds they snagged were woefully insufficient to the amount required.

When the soldiers were given the green light to bring in waterfowl, ducks and geese began disappearing from parks, ponds, and golf courses in startling numbers. Citizens followed suit and trapped as many waterfowl birds as they could find. Some people were making more money selling birds than they made at their jobs.

CHAPTER NINE

Once more the flock of birds had only one thing on their minds. Gotta eat. They were following the Second Los Angeles Aqueduct and had just entered the small burg of Armistead. They had begun to fly north and would follow the aqueduct system all the way to Mono Lake.

They were only vaguely aware of their surroundings. Their hunger was constant now, even when their bellies were full. There was no longer a period in between eating one meal and needing the next. This was different from the disease that initially affected the birds in San Clemente. Perhaps it was the continuous flight or the need to keep moving that distorted their appetites. But whatever the reason, they needed food, and they wanted it now.

Again, the few targets that presented themselves were too fast or too small to chase after so far. They needed something more substantial and slower they could assail together. Only by smothering their prey with their numbers, as they had done with the man at Elk Hills, could they be assured of success.

Nothing was moving below them that fit this pattern. But they knew people lived in these towns, no matter how small. They circled around again and finding no one about veered toward Inyokern to the northwest. Not much bigger than Armistead, there might be something that could sustain them until their next meal.

ᵏ ᵏᵗᵏ ᵏ ᵏᵗᵏ ᵏ ᵏᵗᵏ ᵏ ᵏᵗ ᵏ ᵏᵗᵏ ᵏ ᵏᵗᵏ ᵏ ᵏᵗᵏ

The Los Angeles Aqueduct ran 338 miles from Mono Lake all the way down to the San Fernando Valley in Southern California. There has been tremendous controversy and debate about the system ever since the 1920s, seven short years after its dedication, up to today. Farmers along the Owens Valley had lost the valuable resource they were using to irrigate their farms. In their frustration and anger, protesters went so far as to blow-up portions of the aqueduct initiating the famed "Water Wars."

Even after the 1928 bursting of the St. Francis Dam in Los Angeles County, the water continued to flow through the system. The collapsing dam inundated the towns of Castaic Junction, Fillmore, Bardsdale and Piru with billions of gallons of water. More than 400 residents lost their lives, drowning without warning. After an extensive investigation, it was determined that the rock in the area had been too unstable to support the dam in the first place.

The waterway also significantly reduced the water levels at Mono Lake, causing the tufa limestone edifices to rise up into the towers now seen. For a time, there was a danger of this great natural resource disappearing altogether, along with its tremendous diversity of wildlife. The basin was being sucked dry by the residents of Los Angeles County.

In 1994, the State Water Resources Control Board

amended the licenses for water diversion to the Los
Angeles Department of Water and Power. This decision
set a target elevation for the water level of Mono Lake,
thus establishing the required minimum and peak stream
flowing into the lake and called for specific restoration
activities. Doing this saved Mono Lake.

Most of the land in the Mono Basin is now managed
by the USFS, the State of California, and numerous
other California resources agencies, all involved in
protecting this vital ecosystem from the thirsty people
of Southern California.

The waterfowl at Mono Lake was once in the millions.
Before the drawing down of the lake, and more
importantly, the creeks that brought the freshwater to
the basin. Over 97 percent of the waterfowl that used to
inhabit this area is gone now. There was a time when one
could see Ruddy Ducks, Canada Goose, Gadwalls, and
Mallards, and more than thirty species of the waterfowl
family.

They continue to be an essential part of the two
million or so birds in the Mono Lake basin that come
every year.

ᐠᐟᑫᐟᐠ ᐠᐟᑫᐟᐠᐟ ᐠᐟᑫᐟᐠᐟ ᐠᐟ ᐠᐟᑫᐟᐠᐟ ᐠᐟᑫᐟᐠ ᐠᐟᑫᐟᐠ

Dr. Greenwood got a knock on his door and said,
"Enter."

Dr. Friedman came in and slowly closed the door
behind her. She looked reticent about why she came to
him.

Dr. Greenwood saw her hesitation and coaxed to her,

"Whatever it is you don't want to tell me, you might as well say it and get it over with."

She approached his desk without sitting and said, "We may have been wrong about San Francisco, or at least premature."

"Really? What's happened to change that?" Dr. Greenwood asked.

"We received a call from California Highway Patrol outside of Bakersfield. He had local police officers report that two oil field engineers were killed at an oil pumping station off the Interstate 5 freeway. He thinks that based on the evidence it was birds."

Dr. Friedman went on to explain that the charred bird remains with the first engineer and the condition of the other body on the second. She finished by saying, "Based on this, it seems the birds we are tracking are heading more easterly, and are much further north than we originally thought."

Dr. Greenwood pulled out his maps and looked at the distance between the oil reserve and Los Olivos from the two reports.

He banged his fist on the desk, "Damn. That just took away the one or two days we figured we gained. And if they are as far east as this, then they could still be heading to either the Great Salt or Mono Lakes. If they track north from here, then as we thought before, to San Francisco. I can't tell where they are going based on this. Can you?"

Dr. Friedman shook her head, "No, and it also means that the dead policeman in Los Olivos was most likely caused by a different group of birds. There is no way they would have reached that point on the same day for both events."

"So we have another deadly flock of birds to contend with," said Dr. Greenwood. "This is getting out of control."

"Any word from Cornell or anyone else?" asked Dr. Friedman.

"Not a peep," Dr. Greenwood said as he shook his head. "I was going to call a few people before you knocked."

"I'm sure they would call you if there was any further development," said Dr. Friedman.

"Yes, but this way they know 'Big Brother' is still watching," said Dr. Greenwood.

"Do you want me to send any of our CDC people out to either Los Olivos or the oil field?" asked Dr. Friedman.

"I am afraid right now the best thing we can do is wait to see when another attack is reported, and then we'll play connect the dots," said Dr. Greenwood.

Dr. Friedman nodded and as she headed for the door said, "Something tells me we won't have to wait too long."

"Thanks for the update," said Dr. Greenwood.

"Sorry it wasn't better news," she said as she left.

ᴋᴋᵗᴋ ᴋᴋᵗᴋ ᴋᴋᵗᴋ ᴋᵗ ᴋᴋᵗᴋ ᴋᴋᵗᴋ ᴋᴋᵗᴋ

Paul Sheehan was in a quandary about what to do. As the Mayor of Irvine, he was pleased about all the attention and extra income his city was receiving from the various federal workers and scientists visiting. He also appreciated the growing number of people in the medical and educational fields working on a cure to stem the spreading virus at UCI and UCI Medical Center, all while staying at Irvine's hotels and eating at the city's restaurants.

What he was upset about was the damage and growing injuries occurring to his residents and the people working in the business centers and shops of Irvine. The city itself was a master planned community made up of what they called "villages." Irvine prided itself on having a great many technology and semiconductor-based industries within its boundaries, along with nearly every type of business imaginable.

From his office off Alton Parkway, Sheehan could see Corporate Parkway and several of the important businesses lining that road. He could even see the bustling Jamboree Road from his office. He smiled when he thought of that name. Most people living and working in Irvine had no idea that the Irvine Ranch played host to the 1953 National Boy Scouts of America's Jamboree. Jamboree Road, a major thruway, which now stretches from Newport Beach to the city of Orange, was named in honor of this event.

His smile turned to a frown as he looked at the sky above the offices. There they are again, he thought to himself. He could see a cloud of dark silhouettes circling above the buildings, cars, and pedestrians moving about the town. He couldn't tell what kind of birds they were, but that didn't matter anymore.

All the species were involved by now. The mayor felt it was crazy that the military was bringing more and more birds to the various facilities for testing but could not rid his city of the pests causing problems on the streets and villages in this town.

Paul Sheehan had talked to everyone from the CDC based at the medical center down to anyone in lab coats about the problem. They were empathetic to his concerns, and all said they were doing everything they could but not much more. He was told they were working on a cure for the birds, and they now had a new medication for anyone that was hurt by them. But it was nearly impossible to kill or trap the birds currently infected, without risking injury to civilians.

He was told about the Peregrine Falcons that began all the problems just days ago. It seemed to him that for every day that passed, the situation was made worse with no real solution in sight. He called the governor's office yesterday and complained to the lieutenant governor. She admitted she was also concerned, but that their hands were tied, as this was a Homeland Security situation, and pretty much out of their control.

The lieutenant governor said that if the situation became worse, the governor's office would place Irvine in a state of emergency to receive additional funds from the federal government.

Somehow, thought Sheehan, *that doesn't sound like any kind of a solution.* He thanked the lieutenant governor for her time and hung up.

Irvine was one of the few towns that had their own police department fully funded by the city. The mayor's office and the chief of police were in the same building. Sheehan had spoken with his Chief of Police Mike

Campbell several times during the last few days about the growing trouble. He came down to Campbell's office once more about the cloud of birds looming outside.

The chief told him that he had increased patrols and his force was already working overtime to try and respond to calls and protect the people. He explained to the mayor that most times the attacks came from nowhere, and then the birds were gone as quickly as they appeared. By the time the police arrived on the scene, it was too late to do anything but administer to the victims.

Plus, his police force was being summoned from one side of town to the other with dozens of calls coming in every hour. "We are getting calls every time two or more birds land on a wire in this town," Campbell complained, "It has caused problems dealing with more serious police work. I'm not saying we don't want to protect our citizens, but this has gotten to the point of hysterical paranoia."

Mayor Sheehan nodded his head. "I could have the governor's office call in the national guard if you need more help."

"There are already too many soldiers coming in and out of our town. And what are they bringing us? More birds," scoffed the police chief. "I think, for now, we will handle the situation ourselves. Besides it is not as if the military can come into here with guns blazing at anything that flies."

The mayor got up from his chair and said, "Well, if you change your mind or come up with another plan, you know where to find me."

"I get the feeling you and I are going to wear out the floor to each other's offices before this is over," said the chief of police.

Similar scenarios were taking place in dozens of towns and cities around Southern California, all the way up to Ventura and beyond. All the town officials were asking the same questions and fielding the same worries. Sacramento wasn't able to offer any solution beyond extra help from the California national guard, and that offer was becoming overtaxed.

Governor Newcomb had been fielding calls for the last two days from the President of the United States, ambassadors, and leaders of several nations. All were asking the same questions about how bad the threat from the birds had become and where things stood.

The governor told them all the same thing. Yes, they had a working vaccine. No, they were unable to cure the birds as yet. Yes, he was told they would soon have SARV under control. No, he did not believe this problem would escape California's borders. And yes, there were dozens of companies and universities working on the problem with hundreds, possibly thousands of people by now addressing the issues at hand.

Gov. Newcomb had a hotline to Dr. Greenwood's private mobile phone. He called for an update at least twice a day. He told his office that if a call came from him, or the CDC working in Irvine, he was to be found immediately, even in the bathroom, if necessary.

Depending on how important a person was calling in, the governor had a bank of people assisting his office. Small towns and citizens were patched through to a phone bank. He had another group that had more up to date information handle larger groups and municipalities. And he and his lieutenant governor handled the large cities and essential policymakers from Washington, D.C., and beyond. Most times this worked, but the answers were staying the same for far too long to satisfy the governor.

During their last conversation, Gov. Newcomb told Dr. Greenwood that he could have access to whatever he or his people needed, but he demanded results for it. He blamed the CDC for the botched job in San Clemente and allowing this to become the disaster it was today. The governor wanted heads, and for every call his office received, he wanted an additional person to lose their job. He told Dr. Greenwood and others that he was determined to make this a reality.

He also warned Dr. Greenwood that there was not nearly enough bodies to protect him if something did not happen to resolve this, and damn soon.

Dr. Greenwood had been threatened before and by higher ranking people than the governor of California, but he didn't argue with the man. He knew that it would accomplish nothing. He told the governor he understood and politely hung up.

Dr. Forrester had made a decision of his own. He had

spoken again with Natalie and knew he needed to tend to his wife, no matter what. His conclusion had been made easier once he learned that Cornell, and not UCSD, had redesigned the antivirus to make it safer, and all eyes were on this rival university. He learned this through Dr. Abernathy and not Ellen Revere. That hurt more than the news, itself.

Dr. Forrester knocked on Dr. Friedman's door and was beckoned in. When he told her of his decision, she did everything she could to convince Dr. Forrester to remain in Irvine and continue with trying to develop a workable spray vaccine. She told him that the threat was far from over and explained some of the events that were taking place that others, like Prof. Revere, knew nothing about.

When she finished, Dr. Forrester said, "I understand your problem, but I have to look out for my own wife and what she is going through. I am deeply concerned she will hurt herself or possibly someone else."

"I am not saying don't go to her," said Dr. Friedman, "I am only saying that you need to return after you do. Spend a day or two getting her situation tended to, and then come back and finish your work here."

"As far as I can see, it is pretty much done," said Forrester. "Cornell has a working antivirus, and you have dozens of colleges and companies working on the aerosol. There isn't much I can do to further that end."

"Your mind and every pair of hands helps us get closer to that end," argued Dr. Friedman, "Don't forget that you, Prof. Revere, and Tory McKnight were closest to the problem and the original solution."

"Well, you still have the other two and Cornell is

closest to the final solution, now," countered Dr. Forrester. "I still have my staff at the university and its medical center working day and night. I can check on their progress down there, In fact, I may be more useful at my own facility."

Dr. Friedman saw there would be little to no chance of convincing Dr. Forrester to stay in Irvine, so she consented to his decision and made him promise to do what he could in San Diego.

"If I am satisfied with my wife's progress, and feel I can do more here than there, I will return as quickly as I can," finished Dr. Forrester.

"I will hold you to that," said Dr. Friedman. She shook his hand and wished him luck with Natalie. "I really do care about her, you know."

"Believe me, I know you have a whole lot more on your plate, but thank you for your concern," Dr. Forrester said and then left her office to pack.

Sarah Coventry and Barney were out for their evening stroll. It had been another lovely day in their town, and she had closed up the country store that she owned and was back home. Coventry Market had been a fixture five miles north of Armistead for the last twenty-five years.

Her dad had opened the store back then after retiring from his duties at the nearby China Lake Naval Air Warfare Center. He liked the peace and quiet of Armistead and its surrounding towns. He decided to open the market as he knew it was needed. He also knew his military pension would keep things going for him, and his family, until the market became established.

Sarah had lost her mom almost a decade before, and her dad passed a few years back. She lived in the house she grew up in and loved the townspeople as much as her parents had. The shopkeeper knew nearly every one of the residents from Armistead down south to Inyokern further northwest. Most all had come by regularly, as she had the best stocked market within twenty miles.

Barney was a regular fixture in the store. The little white American Eskimo dog was friendly and often followed visitors in the store getting what pets and caresses they doled out to him. He was nearly ten years old now, and most customers couldn't remember a time he wasn't around "helping" them shop.

They had been out walking for a while. Sarah looked up to see how low the sun was getting and saw them. It was an extensive collection of birds all flying together. They were flying as if looking for something. A moment later Sarah knew what it must be. It was her.

She picked up Barney and ran the rest of the way home. She had barely made it through the door when she heard the first bird hit the door behind her. Her picture window was hit and shuddered several times as one bird after another slammed into it. She was sure it would break, but it continued to hold firm.

She now could hear the squawking of crows and cries from the gulls as if they were trying to figure a way into the house. Barney was barking for all he was worth trying to scare off the uninvited predators. Sarah found her phone and called 911, she was dispatched to the sheriff's office where she could barely explain the trouble she and her dog were in out of fear and the squawking going on outside.

She was told they would get a deputy out there as soon as they could and the concerned voice at the other end advised her to find something she could strike the birds with, in case they got in.

The birds flew in circles around the house. It had been a warm day, and before she left that morning, Sarah had everything closed up tight and left the air conditioner running. No open windows or doors made it virtually impossible for the birds to get in. The smaller birds that had hit the big window and front door and were lying lifeless beneath them. The crows were pecking at the smaller windows and the frames around them with no success. The gulls were perched on the deck in front of the door Sarah ran through, looking for an opening there.

Food was in there, but there appeared no way to get to it quickly. The birds sat atop the roof, screeching and calling to each other in frustration. After several minutes the remains of the entire flock flew off together to search for a more accessible target.

Only when the deputy arrived fifteen minutes later with lights flashing and siren blaring did Sarah dare to venture out. The only thing the deputy could do was bag the dead birds for analysis. There was not so much as a live sparrow to be seen anywhere around them.

CHAPTER TEN

The National Center for Emerging and Zoonotic Infectious Diseases (NCEZID) department of the Center for Disease Control and Prevention was a mouthful to say at parties. The director of this section of the CDC had a monumental task and a great deal of power.

Dr. Patricia Rosenberg held this prestigious title for the last six years. She worked her way up through various branches of the CDC, directing a great many programs during her tenure with the agency. Dr. Rosenberg trained in internal medicine and completed a fellowship in infectious diseases at Harvard after receiving her doctorate in medical medicine. She never looked back after that.

The NCEZID and its seven divisions work with partners throughout the United States and around the world to prevent illness, disability, and death caused by any known infectious diseases. In the past, this included deadly germs like anthrax, Ebola, and now the Super Aviary Rabies Virus or SARV. The seven divisions have almost thirty branches under them with thousands of people made up of a broad spectrum of infectious disease experts.

The fact that Dr. Rosenberg now stood in Dr. Alice Friedman's office in Irvine spoke to the seriousness of the situation at hand. Like Dr. Friedman, she wasn't a tall woman but had the type of stern straight-edge look that could intimidate the tallest man who stood before her. Dr. Rosenberg spoke with a slight Bostonian accent but made herself easily understood. She wore her dark brown hair long and generally tied it in a ponytail.

She was getting a full debrief from Dr. Friedman about the situation. She asked few questions allowing her branch director of the Division of Preparedness and Emerging Infections to finish. When Dr. Friedman concluded, Dr. Rosenberg nodded her head and was quiet at first, analyzing all the information she'd just been given.

After a few moments, Dr. Rosenberg said, "Do you have a clue how many phone calls I have received from other nations besides our own? Not to mention from experts in every field this touches?"

Dr. Friedman said to her superior, "I am sure quite a number."

"Some of them are accusing us of bioterrorism, saying that we are trying to reshape the world to suit the United States," continued Dr. Rosenberg. "And unfortunately, I am hearing nothing from you that gives me hope that we are close to stopping this."

"We do have a working vaccine in injectable form," countered Dr. Friedman, "We are doing everything possible to make a mass distribution aerosol to inoculate the unaffected birds."

"It sounds like by the time you get one, you will have to spray the entire globe," commented Dr. Rosenberg, "Especially the way this virus is spreading. Look at how many points on the map you said birds were attacking. I appreciate your attention to the migrating birds that you are trying to get ahead of in this, but what are we doing about the rest that are causing problems and infecting people and other animals?"

"For right now we are concentrating on the one front," answered Dr. Friedman, "Once that is under control we will begin treating the other birds. Maybe even do this simultaneously if we can make enough of the antitoxin for both."

"You realize by ignoring this other problem, even, for now, you are putting people's lives in danger and may even add to a worsening situation if these birds decide to fly off to God knows where?" asked Dr. Rosenberg.

Dr. Friedman nodded her head and asked, "What do you suggest, doctor?"

Dr. Rosenberg decided to dismiss the tone in Dr. Friedman's voice. She knew that Dr. Friedman was feeling the same pressures that she was under. She said, "Look, Alice, I am not trying to say you aren't doing everything you can to get this under control. But I need you to look at the entire picture and not narrow this down to one set of birds, however urgent that may be."

"When you speak to Dr. Greenwood, you may come away with a different opinion," said Dr. Friedman. "He is convinced that this will result in an unprecedented extinction event if we can't stop these birds."

"This may sound like a long shot," said Dr. Rosenberg, almost more to herself, "Have you tried fighting fire with fire? In other words, why not use aircraft to try and spot the flock from above? We know there are multi-species in the group, and you believe it is made up primarily of gulls. It seems this large squabble of birds might be seen by small aircraft or by helicopters."

"We are talking a tremendous amount of miles," Dr. Friedman said, although she was clearly considering the possibility.

"Maybe not as bad as you think," said Dr. Rosenberg, "You are getting regular reports on their movements and attacks. It would only be a short time before you can narrow it down to a working area. Besides planes can move faster than birds."

"What happens when we think we've found them?" asked Dr. Friedman, already knowing the answer.

"We destroy them so they can't jeopardize any more birds or people," said Dr. Rosenberg.

"I think we need to speak to Dr. Greenwood about this idea. I believe he could get us the necessary resources to work on this," said Dr. Friedman.

ᴋ ᴋᵗᴋ ᴋ ᴋᵗᴋ ᴋ ᴋᵗᴋ ᴋ ᴋᵗ ᴋ ᴋᵗᴋ ᴋ ᴋᵗᴋ ᴋ ᴋᵗᴋ

Dr. Greenwood and Dr. Rosenberg welcomed each other with a brief hug and Dr. Greenwood said, "My God, Pat, you look great! I swear you never age a day when I see you. I'll bet you have spoken with as many calm, patient souls as I have lately. I guess Dr. Friedman has brought you up to date?"

Dr. Rosenberg had a smile that Dr. Friedman had never seen before. "You two obviously know each other," Dr. Friedman said, "so I'll leave you both..."

Dr. Rosenberg grabbed her arm gently as she went to leave saying, "No, don't leave, Alice. Dr. Greenwood and I have had to deal with multiple issues in the past. He and I have 'saved the world' so to speak a few times, together including the last anthrax scare."

"And we need to do so again," said Dr. Greenwood. "And this time I really do mean the whole world. This is a far more desperate situation than anything we have dealt with before, Pat."

"Okay, Henry, before you go all doom and gloom on me, let's figure out where we stand and what we can do that we haven't tried, yet," said Dr. Rosenberg.

"Dr. Rosenberg may have an idea on stopping our migrating birds," said Dr. Friedman.

Dr. Greenwood raised his eyebrows and looked at Dr. Rosenberg, "What took you so long? Well, what have you got?"

Dr. Rosenberg barely got the idea out into the open and Dr. Greenwood was picking up the phone. "I can't believe I didn't think of that. That's so easy and positively brilliant. Let's just hope these suckers are hiding in plain sight."

"Do you know where to start looking?" asked Dr. Rosenberg.

"Two places come to mind," answered Dr. Greenwood.

"Yes, Los Olivos and Elk Hills Oil Reserve," said Dr. Friedman.

Dr. Greenwood nodded his head and then said into the phone, "Yes, I need Charley Stantis, director of the FAA."

The frustration and anger of the birds were intense

after their failed attempt on Sarah Coventry. Now they
had become genuinely desperate in their search for food
and were snapping at each other in flight. The gulls and
crows were outpacing the smaller birds who were
fighting to keep up. Even the remaining shearwaters
were struggling to fly fast enough to suit the gulls. They
were on a mission. Gotta eat, gotta EAT.

They saw a farm ahead of them and could see that
there were goats in one of the fields. They circled once
allowing the other birds to catch up. They chose a target,
and the gulls led the charge followed by the crows and a
sharp-shinned hawk that was flying with the flock. They
hit a young goat with a flurry of birds. One of the other
goats tried fending the other birds off but was pecked
and jabbed until it retreated.

As angry as the birds had become, nothing was going
to prevent them from eating. They had the goat pinned
to the ground and was pecking at the soft tissues while
the hawk was tearing at the hide of the goat. The goat
bleated its cries while the rest of the herd stood by
helplessly, watching one its members get ripped to shreds
and devoured before their eyes. Several of the goats ran
off fearing the same fate happening to them.

The savagery continued for another hour until
nothing remained of the goat worth trying to eat. The
birds stood around for another fifteen minutes until they
could fly again after their large dinner.

ᐠ ᐟᐟᐠ ᐟᐠ ᐟᐠᐟ ᐠ ᐠ ᐠ ᐟ ᐠ ᐟᐠ ᐟᐠᐟᐠ ᐟᐠ ᐟᐠ ᐠ ᐟᐠᐟ

Charley Stantis put out a bulletin to every airport

and landing strip from Bakersfield, California, to Las Vegas, Nevada, and all the way north to Sacramento. Any private plane pilots were to be on the lookout for a flock of birds made up of various types, most notably seagulls. He and Dr. Greenwood agreed that a reward of $10,000 for the correct location would make sure those not planning a trip soon were given sufficient motivation to get their craft into the air.

Stantis also made sure the FAA alerted medivacs, news channels, and privateers with helicopters about the search and locate details. They were told not to engage or disrupt the birds in any way but to report and continue to track the group for as long as possible.

Stantis conservatively thought this could put as many as five hundred or more pairs of eyes into the sky to find the culprits that had caused all the trouble in Southern California. He also secretly guessed this might be a needle in a haystack, as it was a lot of ground to cover. Even with that many pilots looking, they may not find the flock they sought. Or worse, it could result in too many reports to investigate efficiently, and still not see the birds they needed. Not to mention they were seeking a moving target, and no one was sure where they were moving to.

Stantis was coordinating any civilian pilot's reports with the various air force bases in central and northern California, including Vandenberg, Travis, and the Naval Air Weapons Station in China Lake. These bases were on alert if the offending birds were found. It would be the military's responsibility to stop them from proceeding any further.

ʞ ʞ⁺ʞ ʞ ʞ⁺ʞ ʞ ʞ⁺ʞ ʞ⁺ ʞ ʞ⁺ʞ ʞ ʞ⁺ʞ ʞ ʞ⁺ʞ

As Stantis was working on establishing his network, Dr. Friedman received a call from the California Highway Patrol. The moment she got off the call she walked into the newly occupied office of Dr. Rosenberg and asked her to accompany her to Dr. Greenwood's office.

A moment later both women stood before Dr. Greenwood's desk. Dr. Friedman reported on the call she had received.

"I got a call from Highway Patrol, they reported two strange incidents. The first was that a woman was attacked by a 'huge number of birds' as she called it north of Red Rock Canyon Park off California Route 14. Also, they said a farmer filed a complaint that one of his goats was killed and butchered in the middle of a field. He said there was nothing left but bones and a hide."

"That sounds like it could be our group," Dr. Greenwood said as he consulted his map again. "Yeah, that would make sense if you follow it up from the Elk Hills incident, it looks like they are heading east and then north on the leeward side of the Sierras."

"That would probably mean they are heading for either Mono or the Great Salt Lake," said Dr. Friedman.

"If I had to guess," said Dr. Rosenberg, "I would bet on Mono Lake and concentrate there."

"Why is that, Pat?" asked Dr. Greenwood.

"Because Mono is a whole lot closer, and if they are

headed there, you need to get your spraying done in time. And if it is Great Salt, they would have to fly many more days to reach it. So I would concentrate on Mono. That is assuming we don't hunt them down first."

"Are you going to call your friend at the FAA?" asked Dr. Friedman.

"Stantis already has the word out, and is busy creating his network," said Dr. Greenwood. "I think I will give him some time. Besides, are we seriously thinking a goat should determine our next move? That worries me and makes me think we are grasping at straws. I would really like more concrete evidence than a near miss with a woman and that."

"It's the most relevant reports we have heard since the oil reserve incident," said Dr. Friedman, "There aren't a whole lot of people in that area to corroborate anything. It's not like here in Irvine."

"Pretty soon it is not going to matter where you look, you are going to have problems from these damn birds everywhere," said Dr. Rosenberg. "I would go with what you have, and if they are out there, the sparse population will give us a better opportunity to get rid of them without civilian interference or injury."

Dr. Greenwood nodded and rubbed his head. "Okay, I will call Stantis and tell him to pull whatever strings he has to get some eyes out there and see if they can locate them. Thanks for the heads-up Dr. Friedman."

The women left him to make his call.

꙳꙳꙳꙳꙳꙳꙳꙳꙳꙳꙳꙳꙳꙳꙳꙳꙳꙳

The branches of the giant dead tree in Lake Forest held nearly seventy-five birds of almost a dozen species. The original twelve vultures were still there, but they had been joined by other vultures, crows, hawks, owls, mockingbirds, ravens, a couple blue jays, and even a bald eagle.

At its base were birds that didn't perch in trees. California Gulls, sandpipers, plovers, shearwaters and the like were huddled around squawking and nudging each other as if trying to get them to fly. Hours before, a semitrailer truck struck a good-size doe and threw her to the side of the Interstate 5 freeway. It was just far enough from the ever-busy highway for the birds to converge on the dead deer and feed without danger of being hit by traffic themselves.

After that large meal, they returned to roost, but still felt the need to eat again. The birds' hunger was never satisfied. A few of the birds in this group actually died from overeating. Their organs became overexerted from all the food they consumed, and their stomachs exploded. Other birds with the SAR virus suffered the same fate in other areas.

As they gathered in and around the tree, they screeched, squawked, and called to each other sounding like a frenzied mob gathering. The sound could be heard a quarter mile away, but the tree stood at the edge of a small lake just outside the residential community, so it didn't attract any attention.

This was more advantageous to the residents than the birds. The birds would have blitzed any curiosity seekers wandering near enough to garner the flock's focus.

The congress of birds seemed to be planning another raid and were squawking a great deal, as if discussing where to go next. This flock also had scouts flying around the area scoping out possible food caches. So far, they hadn't needed to attack moving prey, as the scouts found enough carcasses to feed off of keeping the group satiated. This was becoming less and less the case as the population of the group continued to increase.

Groups were also forming in Huntington Beach, Long Beach, Santa Monica, Thousand Oaks, Ventura, and of course, Irvine. The numbers were as small as thirty to as large as the several hundred that occupied the Bowerman landfill before they became trapped by the military. The soldiers removed one hundred twenty-eight birds, but the remainder were gathering new birds to their group daily.

As each assemblage developed and grew, it became bolder and more hostile. Many beaches and parks were closed off from the public to prevent the birds from attacking pedestrians. The CDC had requested all the communities from San Diego to San Luis Obispo to be vigilant of birds grouping together and to ward off any residents from getting too close to the gathering birds.

Some communities tried to trap the birds and destroy them, but the birds would fly off together before they could get close enough. The birds would begin "talking" to each other as soon as a movement toward them was noticed. They would fly off in every direction leaving no more than a couple birds heading off together. If they were able to catch any birds, it was never more than one or two out of the dozens or more that had gathered moments before.

The communities warned residents not to take matters into their own hands. They were beginning to receive reports of gunfire, and the police were not taking these perpetrators lightly. Anyone caught discharging a weapon in their respective community won themselves a quick trip to the local jail. If anybody felt they were under threat of a bird attack, they were advised to call 911 and report it, period.

People had begun walking their dogs shorter distances, most stayed within their own small plots of land. Inhabitants would fight over close parking spaces because of the fear of a bird attack walking across the parking lot. Stores and shops were nearly empty of patrons, and even grocery stores had fewer people shopping in them. Those that did venture out would fill their shopping cart to the brim. Bread, water, milk, and snack items disappeared from the shelves and could not be restocked fast enough.

Southern California had become lock-jawed into a state of fear. There were still many birds that were unaffected by the disease, but they were eyed with the same suspicion and worry as the gathering offenders. There was one community that seemed safe from all this. The town where all this began, San Clemente, was being called a "Bird Free Zone" by residents of other communities.

This did not make San Clemente popular with the other towns along the south coast. Especially, since the whole problem they experienced began with this town. However, San Clemente was filled with visitors once more. Aside from a few seagulls and pelicans floating offshore in the surf and deemed "safe," there were almost no birds to be seen. This was a welcome sight to visitors from other towns. The shops and restaurants were bustling, and the owners were smiling as broadly as the patrons. Things were, at last, returning to normal here.

People also drove further south to places like Oceanside, and as far down as San Diego. They had learned from the news sources and social media posts that nowhere north or east of them was any safer than their own town. A good many residents traveled this far south to shop. Popular markets and box stores that they usually frequented in their own neighborhood were now filled to bursting from the visiting shoppers. There they could walk around the parking lots without winged attackers charging them from above.

Fortunately, most of the schools were still out for the summer. This did help curtail some of the populace from traveling around in the morning and afternoon. Other residents did their marketing late at night, believing they were safer as generally speaking, birds rarely flew at night. A few of these misguided souls forgot about owls and learned the hard way that infected birds scavenged all hours for food sources.

Some of the colleges canceled their scheduled summer classes to protect their students and teachers from possible bombardments. They were also being run by skeleton crews when reasonable, to protect their staff. Many colleges were situated on large parcels, and it would not be able to cover the grounds safely if birds were about. A few persons had been struck by a bird or two as proof of their concerns.

Other towns and mayors like Paul Sheehan were desperately trying to convince their residents to remain indoors and stay off the streets as much as possible. Some towns had even taken to posting local police at the bigger stores and shopping centers as a show of force to protect residents. These police officers were warned not to draw their firearms, and to use caution if any birds were sighted but not to overreact. The town leaders told them this would ensure more panic and concern, not to mention someone might get hurt.

ĸ ⱦ ⱦ ⱦ ĸ ⱦ ⱦ ⱦ ĸ ⱦ ⱦ ⱦ ĸ ⱦ ⱦ ĸ ⱦ ⱦ ⱦ ĸ ⱦ ⱦ ⱦ ĸ ⱦ ⱦ ⱦ

Captain John Torelli climbed into the cockpit of his Boeing AH-64 Apache helicopter. His co-pilot and gunner, Lieutenant Tim "Preacher" Churchill was already preparing the twin turbo-shaft copter for flight. Capt. Torelli's call sign was "Snake Pit" because running into him and his Apache, was like falling into a nest of vipers.

They were stationed at the Naval Air Warfare Station in China Lake, California. The NAWS is the United States Navy's most significant single landholding, representing 85 percent of the Navy's land for weapons and armaments research, development, acquisition, testing and evaluation (RDAT&E) use. It comprises 38 percent of the Navy's land holdings worldwide. In total, its two ranges and main site cover more than 1,100,000 acres, an area larger than the state of Rhode Island.

Capt. Torelli and the Lt. Churchill had orders to

locate and "obliterate a flock of birds that was carrying a world-threatening disease before they could infect any other life form." The men ran through their checklist and fired up the helicopter.

The copter lifted off from its pad and headed to the last reported possible area where the goat was attacked. Both men had been fully briefed on the birds' movements and known attacks. They were also advised to use caution destroying the birds, and not be tainted by the birds or their blood, as they would have to undergo rabies treatment if they did.

They headed south toward Armistead. The two latest reports put the targets north of the town. The first being a few miles north off the highway and the farm incident being just south of Freeman Junction, an old ghost town that had died back in 1976. The place used to be a stagecoach stop in the latter 1800s. During the time of the stagecoach stop, several freight wagons and one stagecoach had been robbed. It went out of business shortly after opening. After that, a few diners and later a gas station opened up along with a few other businesses. All of which dried up and moved away. All that remained was the Los Angeles Aqueduct and a historical marker.

There was not much to see around this part of California. The entire area was basically a desert with a few tumbleweeds rolling around and the mountains in the distance. Snake Pit brought the craft to a higher elevation allowing them to notice any movement below them. They saw a total of three cars moving along the highway and nothing more. The pilot lowered the copter to his original bearing and headed again toward Armistead cruising slowly.

The airmen searched the area between Los Angeles Aqueduct Road and Highway 14 in the vicinity of Homestead and Inyokern, California. They did not see anything beyond a few songbirds, and certainly no groups of birds. They circled around once more and then returned to base after checking in to see if any new reports came in.

The birds were there. They decided to roost because they were having trouble flying from all the food they had ingested combined with the heat of the day. There was an old deserted barn that provided shade. The birds were resting in there for the time being. They heard the helicopter fly by twice and paid it no mind.

к к⁺к к к⁺к к к⁺к к⁺к к⁺к к к⁺к к⁺к к к⁺к

When Dr. Forrester returned home, he found the place a shambles. Dishes were smashed on the floor, clothes strewn all around the house. And his home office was trashed with papers thrown everywhere. His wife wasn't home, and at first, Forrester thought his house might have been burglarized. Closer inspection told him this had not been the case.

He began by cleaning up the broken and unwashed dishes in the sink. He took all the trash out and then started collecting his wife's clothes. He wasn't sure if they were clean or dirty, so he neatly stacked them on their bed to sort later.

He went to his office and tried to assess what Natalie

might have been looking for in there. He couldn't imagine, so he began picking up and organizing his files once more. He had almost collected everything when he heard a key in the lock and the front door open. He came out of the office to see a disheveled version of his wife standing before him.

"What are you doing here?" she said warily. "Had enough of your strumpets up north?"

Forrester approached his wife to give her a hug, but she pushed him back. "So what is the story? Are you just here to change out clothing, or get some more of your important personal papers?"

"I came home to see my wife, who obviously needs my help," answered Dr. Forrester softly.

"I don't need your goddamned help. I am doing just fine, thank you," Natalie snarled.

"So I saw," commented Dr. Forrester, "I thought the house had been burgled when I came in."

Dr. Forrester was still treading lightly, but he was also frustrated to drive all the way home like a madman, only to meet a person who clearly didn't care that he was there. He fought back his feelings, realizing that his wife was very ill, and that was the real reason he was standing there now.

Natalie ignored him and went to the bedroom slamming the door behind her. After a few minutes, he walked over to the door and said to his wife on the other side, "I thought we'd take a ride since it is so nice a day and you could tell me what has been going on while I've been gone?"

She did not immediately respond. Dr. Forrester had

called his doctor's office, and after talking to three different people and being put on hold for twenty minutes, he finally got to speak with his doctor. He had told him about Natalie's condition and the root cause of it. The doctor told him he had a few patients suffering from this malady and had pretty good success with two particular medications.

The doctor said that since Natalie was so uncooperative, he would call in the prescriptions and he could set up a follow-up appointment once she was more like herself. Dr. Forrester thanked him, told him what pharmacy to contact and then hung up. He had planned to stop at the pharmacy to pick up the medications but wanted to get home too badly to waste time waiting at the drug store.

He thought maybe the two of them could go together. He heard her changing through the door, but she still did not answer him. He asked again and saw the door swing open before him.

"Why in the hell would I want to go with you anywhere?" she snapped, "You left me without barely a thought, and now you want to go riding around? What are you up to anyway?"

"I have a couple errands to run, and I am out of one of my medications, so I figured we would just go together," said Forrester as innocently as possible.

"Oh! So that's it. I was a convenient stop for you to get your pills and more clothes," cried Natalie. "I should've known it was nothing more than that."

"Oh, Judas Priest, Nat! For the love of Pete, can't we just talk for a little bit without all the nastiness?"

complained Dr. Forrester losing his patience. "Please put away all these delusions and accusations. I came to see you and spend some time together, but I do not know how long I can stay. There are some severe issues still taking place. I had to leave a lot of things hanging to get here."

Natalie still seemed unemotional about his arrival, but then said in a softer voice, "Okay, I am still quite upset, but let's say I give you the benefit of the doubt. How long are you here for this time?"

"I don't know, as long as I can be. I have a few things I can do at the university for them, which I hope will help me remain here longer and be with you," said Dr. Forrester.

Natalie stood there staring at him for a moment and then blinked. "How about I make us a cup of coffee, and we can talk first. Besides aren't you tired of driving?"

Oh my God, thought Dr. Forrester, *It is like someone threw a switch and she's back. She is acting like my old Nat again.*

"How about a hug hello, first," he asked.

"Don't push it," she said, but then walked to him and gave him a brief hug.

"I have an idea," Dr. Forrester said. "How about I take you to that coffee shop you like so much? The pharmacy is close by there, and we could kill two birds with one stone?"

"Only if you promise not to mention birds like you just did," said a tense Natalie, "I am so sick of that subject I could scream!"

Dr. Forrester heard her voice rising and held up his

hand quickly, "I promise, absolutely no mention of it. Now let's go before everyone leaves work and gets there before us."

They did not talk too much on the way there. Dr. Forrester's entire world was revolving around the birds and what he was working on to stem the threats taking place. Apparently, Natalie did not have much to say either.

Dr. Forrester asked her about her classes and other teachers at the university, but her answers were cryptic or short and concise, at best. They discussed the weather a little, which had been typical for that time of year, and not much more. Dr. Forrester was scared to bring up her feelings because he was sure it might set her off again. They mostly rode to the coffee shop in silence.

Once there, Natalie ordered something unusual. She requested a much bolder blend than her regular coffee. Dr. Forrester got his preferred cup, and they sat down. "That's stronger than what you usually drink, do you like that better now?"

Natalie seemed to take offense at his question and barked, "Now you don't like what kind of coffee I drink?"

Again Dr. Forrester threw up his hands in defense and said quickly, "No. Nat, that's fine, I usually order the stronger blends. I am happy to see you enjoy them now, too. We could enjoy them together at home more often was my thought."

Natalie settled down again, and Dr. Forrester thought how he couldn't wait to get the pills from the pharmacy. He was still trying to figure out a way to get them into his wife without a major battle. He was hoping they were small in size.

Tory McKnight was feeling tired and strained. Before, when she was working on this problem in San Clemente, she had felt like she was an integral part of the team. Now she felt more like a more common lab assistant than someone helping solve this crisis.

She supposed that maybe fame came too quickly and easily to her. Especially after helping develop the vaccine that was named after her. She was the happiest she had ever been during those last days in San Clemente. She had Chris Palmer, a real-life hero as her boyfriend, the admiration of her two professors, and was moving to Cornell from UCSD at the request of one of the best-known persons in the field of ornithology. She was even proud of the fact that she was the person who had gotten Prof. Revere and Dr. Forrester together to work on the bird attacks in the first place.

And now Dr. Forrester had returned to San Diego to care for his wife, Natalie. Tory liked Natalie but was disappointed that he wasn't with "the team" here in Irvine. She was sure they were getting close to resolving the situation. Tory was more concerned about that then having a vaccine in her name, but it stung to think the McKnight vaccine would be called something else upon its completion.

Prof. Revere had taught Tory something very few people knew. Tory was trained to draw cerebrospinal fluid from birds. It was a delicate procedure and could not even be accomplished by many veterinary specialists, let alone a grad student. Anesthetizing the bird after having it fast for twelve hours was tough enough, the spinal tap itself was almost the more straightforward part of the procedure as the bird was motionless, and that was anything but easy.

It was something Tory was becoming very adept at, as she had done it many times by now. It was the only way to determine whether or not the bird was infected without destroying the animal thoroughly. It was also necessary to determine if the virus was present after vaccinating the bird.

She was all ready and packed to leave for Cornell. She even had other grad students in New York seeking an apartment for her, which would be covered under her scholarship arrangement. Tory was concerned if she would ever get the chance to move there if they did not get this epidemic under control in time. If the outbreak occurred as Dr. Greenwood spoke of, there would be little reason to move anywhere.

But Tory was an optimist. She knew that somehow they would get this under control. She had already heard the whispers about them hunting down the offending birds, and was seeing firsthand how many infected birds were being brought into the lab. Thankfully, many of these were being moved to other testing sights around the country.

Her relationship with Chris had cooled, but they still spoke many evenings, and she was glad to have someone else to talk with about everything she was doing. It was also refreshing to listen to his routine and what he was seeing in the medical center or during his lifeguard duties to take her mind off of her state of affairs.

There was still a tension when they talked due to the overall pall concerning the events that continued unabated. Chris was more vocal concerning the future, and the futility of it, if things kept progressing in the direction they were going. Tory tried to reassure him the worst would not come to pass. Tory was not sure whether she was trying to convince Chris, or herself, with her comments.

She told Chris information that she was sure was confidential. Tory made Chris promise not to tell anyone else except his roommate, Steve. Mostly because Chris and Steve owned their house together and had been friends for many years. She figured Chris would need an outlet for his concerns just as she had required Chris. Tory felt the necessity to get things "off her chest" and felt if she couldn't tell him she might explode.

They were trying to figure a time to get together. Tory felt she needed to lay in his arms and be reassured everything was going to be okay. But with her working eleven and twelve hours a day, and Chris doing the same, it was difficult at best to reunite even for a night.

They tabled trying to get together until Tory could break away for longer. Currently, without Dr. Forrester to assist Prof. Revere, Tory knew that the professor would need more of Tory's time than less. If, as she felt, this would all resolve itself in the end, she and Prof. Revere would be spending a great deal of time together at Cornell over the next couple years. She wasn't about to jeopardize their relationship, not even to be with Chris.

CHAPTER ELEVEN

The next morning Snake Pit and Preacher and their helicopter were up earlier in the morning. They resumed their search starting around the goat ranch and moved north in a zigzag pattern going east and west.

The birds were on the move as well. About an hour before the helicopter left the China Lake facility, the birds had flown by the base about five miles west. They were searching once more for food, but also seemed more determined to make progress to Mono Lake. They were almost to the Coso Rest Area off U.S. Highway 395 when they were spotted.

Preacher saw them first as the birds were off below him and to the right of the cockpit. When Snake Pit brought the copter further to starboard, he could see them, too. It had to be their target. There were about forty birds of varying types flying together. From their distance, it was hard to make out exact species, but they could see black, white, and brown birds and could tell the shape of gulls that were more distinct than the others.

Snake Pit activated the chain gun and initiated the Integrated Helmet and Display Sighting System. This allowed Snake Pit to slave the weapon to his helmet, so wherever he looked the gun would follow. The AH-64's standard of performance for aerial gunnery is to achieve at least 1 hit for every 30 shots fired at a wheeled vehicle from a range of 870–1,300 yards. He was hoping to do a lot better with the birds.

He told Preacher to take the controls and looked around to make sure there were no civilians in the area. Upon seeing nothing moving, he returned his focus on the birds. They were now within about one hundred yards of the birds, and Snake Pit took aim as Preacher brought the copter on a level altitude matching the birds.

The birds were still flying in a fairly tight group. Not wingtip to wingtip but close. Crows, gulls, and shearwaters led the pack with smaller birds staying as close as they could. The more massive wings of the leaders were able to fly faster than the others, but they were gliding a lot to allow the other birds to keep up. They had not noticed the copter closing in on them until the last moment.

Snake Pit took one last look at his bearings and fired. The chain gun spit its first hundred rounds at the targets before it. One bird was struck and the rest of the birds dissolved into nearly forty different directions. Some birds dove for the hard-deck below them, others flew straight up, and the rest flew off in every direction on the compass.

Preacher pulled the helicopter hard to port as he tried to follow the most significant number of birds heading in one direction. Snake Pit saw the birds veering left and turned toward them. He fired another burst, but the shots went right as the birds banked left. He turned his head more but as quick as he could turn his head, they were faster and would reverse their course.

The other birds had scattered to the four winds, and now there were barely even a pair of birds heading in the same direction. Preacher asked his pilot if he should go higher to see if the birds would gather again.

Snake Pit returned the gun to hand controlled Target Acquisition and Designation System or TADS so he could take back the controls to the copter. He ordered Preacher to take the gun while he took a look around for their quarry. He flew the helicopter in a circle and could only see an occasional bird flying off in the direction that was not worth pursuing.

"Any suggestions?" asked Snake Pit.

"Maybe we should ask the base?" answered Preacher.

They contacted the base and told them that they had made contact with their mission targets, but they had "evaded destruction" by heading off from the fight.

Major Tom Christie asked the crew where the targets were currently.

"Everywhere and nowhere, sir," said Snake Pit.

"Pilot, can you be a little more specific?" asked Major Christie.

"They flew off in multiple directions and elevations. They have not returned to our vector," answered the pilot.

"What is your fuel status?" asked the major.

"We are still pretty full up, major. We could stay up here for a couple hours easily." answered the captain.

"Then I suggest you do just that," replied Maj. Christie. "They may return to their original flight pattern, which suggests they are heading more north-northeast."

"Aye, aye, Major," responded Snake Pit. "We will keep you apprised of our situation."

"Control out," came over the headset and then switched off.

"Guess we are on a joyride for a spell," said Preacher.

One bird. All that for one goddamned bird, thought Snake Pit. He started to think of a better plan for when they ran into the birds again.

ᛕ ᛕ

The switchboard at the UCI Medical Center received a phone call. The receptionist answered, and the voice at the other end said, "I need to talk with the highest ranking person in the CDC that is there."

"And may I ask who is calling and your purpose, please?" asked the receptionist as patiently as possible.

"This is the CEO of Synergistic Pharmaceuticals, and I can promise you that they will want to talk with me, immediately," answered the voice.

The phone rang in Dr. Patricia Rosenberg's office. She picked it up and told the receptionist, "Okay, yes, patch him through."

A moment later Dr. Rosenberg said, "This is Dr. Pat Rosenberg, and I am the Director of the NCEZID for the CDC, how may I help you?"

"This is Dave Bugalski, CEO of Synergistic Pharmaceuticals, and we have a working aerosol spray vaccine for the SAR virus."

ᛕ ᛕ

The gulls were still heading north as expected. But now they were flying mostly solo, avoiding the other birds in the flock. It was as if they had planned for this eventuality and were doing this on command. The other birds like the crows and ravens were also dispersed throughout the desert floor. Some were in the foothills to the west, others flew over the highway at various elevations and in front or back of the surrounding birds in the area.

They remained as spread out as possible to make themselves an insignificant target, nearly impossible to shoot. The California Gulls seemed renewed in getting to their summer grounds and were flying harder and faster than they had before. They now seemed less interested in the other birds that had accompanied them, and they even ignored the growing hunger that seemed never to leave them.

They had to get to their own kind to mingle and mix with the other seagulls. They were being hunted, and they knew the sooner they got to Mono Lake, the better their chances stood at being safe among their own numbers. They had made it to Sykes and were heading directly for Tallus and Dunmovin.

As long as it seemed safe to do so, the gulls would gather up once more at the South Haiwee Reservoir as they had stopped there in years past. Often they had met other gulls heading to Mono there, and the increased flock would fly up together. This year they were much later at arriving at the reservoir than in years past.

Maybe they might even find something there to eat.

The other birds were flying about as if confused and not knowing which direction to head toward. Many of the birds headed to the hills and landed in the first trees and scrub bushes they came across. There they waited to see if the other birds would gather up again. Unlike the gulls, they did not have a planned destination and were flying with the gulls mostly to get food.

With the gulls, crows, and ravens all scattered, they were not sure what to do next. They were hungry, but without the larger birds around to help them secure food, they were not sure how they would eat. Outside of an occasional insect or two, they were too small to capture their own meals and knew this would not suffice their current state of hunger.

They were changed. Their instincts had short-circuited, and their brains were not functioning as they had before. The virus changed everything about their patterns and the way they operated. These birds began to panic and were singing and screeching beyond anything they had ever done before. These calls for help went unanswered.

ᴋ ᴋ ᴋ ᴋ ᴋ ᴋ ᴋ ᴋ ᴋ ᴋ ᴋ ᴋ ᴋ ᴋ ᴋ ᴋ ᴋ ᴋ ᴋ

Last night had been a very bumpy ride for Dr. Forrester and his wife. Somehow, Forrester had managed to get his wife in the pharmacy, and while she did a little shopping of her own for some personal items, he got her pills and renewed a prescription for himself in case she asked to see what he came to get.

He managed to get the necessary dosage into a glass

of wine that evening. After a few sips, Natalie said the
wine had turned sour and threw at least half the
contents down the drain, along with the rest of the
bottle. The remainder of the evening was like dancing
around a live wire. Sometimes Natalie was more like her
old self, but just as quickly she would turn on him and
start yelling about what a horrible husband he was for a
variety of reasons, both real and imagined.

Forrester had been guilty of running off ever since he
received that first phone call from Tory McKnight in San
Clemente. He brought Natalie with him to try and make
up for it, but she was injured at the Pier Massacre which
had brought on all the current troubles he was facing
now. The rest was pretty much in Natalie's mind and
nowhere else.

He asked her to try some medication at breakfast,
and she launched into a new tirade about how he was
trying to drug her and wanted to kill her so he could run
off with his "other women." Forrester thought
momentarily about forcing the pills down her throat,
after all, they were just two little pills but realized what
he might have to go through to accomplish this feat. He
decided to try a different tact similar to the wine.

Natalie had a class she needed to teach at the
university that day. Forrester said he also needed to
check into the medical unit about how they were
proceeding with the vaccine and offered to drive her. Her
hackles were still up, but she finally agreed to the idea.

Once there, he knew that Nat liked coffee while she
taught. Forrester offered to get her the coffee from the
cafeteria and ground the pills into the steaming brew. He

got another for himself and took them to her office.

Without saying a word, Nat took the coffee and her lesson planner and walked off to her class.

Dr. Forrester went over to the medical building and talked with the doctors that were working on the vaccine and a cure for the first batch administered. They had received the new vaccine from Cornell and were still trying to make an airborne version of it. So far they were not close to perfecting it.

The second project they were nearer a solution, but not ready to put it out as yet. They were still testing to make sure there were no other side effects or problems. Forrester said as soon as they were ready, he had a test subject for them. *Albeit unwilling,* he thought to himself.

ᛚ ᛚ⁺ᛚ ᛚ ᛚ⁺ᛚ ᛚ ᛚ⁺ᛚ ᛚ⁺ᛚ ᛚ ᛚ⁺ᛚ ᛚ ᛚ⁺ᛚ ᛚ ᛚ⁺ᛚ

Dr. Greenwood was on his way to Dr. Rosenberg's office. When he got there, he found Rosenberg there with Drs. Friedman and Abernathy. Dr. Rosenberg looked at him and said, "Good, I was just going to call you and ask you to join us."

"Oh? What's happening?" asked Dr. Greenwood.

"Well I have good news," said Dr. Rosenberg.

"Please give it to me, my day hasn't been that great," Dr. Greenwood said sourly.

"We have a successful airborne derivative of the SARV vaccine through Synergistic Pharma," said Dr. Rosenberg.

"Well," said Dr. Greenwood, "That is good news. I had just gotten off the phone with a bunch of people, and I was coming here to tell you that my orders from on high are to use whatever we have today to stem the spread of the disease. The timing of this could not be better. How soon can we manufacture it for use in the field?"

"Maybe four or five days," answered Dr. Abernathy, "It would take us that long to manufacture enough of it to cover the areas we are looking at."

"I don't think we have that long, but I'll get back to that in a moment. I have some news, but it is not good. An attack helicopter found our migrating flock of birds, but they only managed to scatter them like confetti thrown at a fan," said Dr. Greenwood. "They haven't seen so much as a feather since then. However they did get a bearing, and it appears you and Dr. Friedman were right, Pat. They seem to be heading to Mono."

"At least that's some good news," said Dr. Abernathy. "It is smaller and easier to cover with the new pathogen."

"Yes, but based on where they spotted the birds, and the remaining distance to Mono Lake, we do not have four or five days, Grant," replied Dr. Greenwood, "My estimation puts us at two, at most three, if we are lucky. And we'd have to be extremely lucky. That is why I was ordered to go with what we already have in the works."

"I have a dozen places standing by that can begin manufacturing the vaccine as soon as we get it to them. Many of these are not to great a distance from Synergistic," said Dr. Friedman. "We could be up and running on that front in a matter of hours."

"Do we have Synergistic's cooperation for that?"

asked Dr. Abernathy.

"I made it clear to Mr. Bugalski that this was a national emergency, and that his company would be expected to cooperate in every way possible, especially if he wants that gold ring at the end of this carousel," said Dr. Rosenberg.

"We have a lot of work to do and not much time to do it," said Dr. Greenwood. "Pat, you and your team get that vaccine manufactured. I will get the planes fueled up and ready at Travis, as I was about to do, and I need to call all those I just hung up with and tell them the change in plans."

"Grant, you come with me and help me get hold of the potential manufacturing facilities," said Dr. Friedman and they left the office.

Dr. Rosenberg looked at Dr. Greenwood and smiled, "Time to save the world, again."

"I pray we do," replied Dr. Greenwood. He gave her forearm a squeeze and left her office.

᛭ ᛭

Snake Pit knew that the compartment and rotor blades of his Apache AH-64 were designed to sustain hits from 23-millimeter rounds. The airframe included nearly 2,500 pounds of protection and had a self-sealing fuel system to protect against ballistic projectiles. If he could face a combat scenario like that, then he knew he could do more damage to birds then they could do to them.

The next time he saw the birds together, he would fly

directly into them. Thinking how well he was protected sitting up and behind Preacher, he thought knocking some birds out of the sky with his rotor blades would not even scratch the edges of the helicopter. Further, the frame was sealed tight to prevent getting bloodied themselves.

He was still flying around in concentric circles heading further north. He went a little further with each pass and was now near Talus. He saw a couple crows flying together but wasn't sure if that was part of the flock he sought or just random birds flying. Neither he nor Preacher, saw any birds flying in a group, whether the same species or not.

They were beginning to get low on fuel, and after checking in with their base once more, they headed back to refuel.

↞↞↟↞ ↞↞↟↞↞↞↟↞ ↞↟↞ ↞↞↟↞↞↞↟↞ ↞↞↟↞

As each of the migrating birds flew past Dunmovin, they headed north-northeast to the South Haiwee Reservoir they could see just ahead of them. They were looking for others of their kind and began gathering up once more near the shore of the reservoir.

A dozen years ago the Los Angeles Department of Water and Power closed the reservoir to the public. So not a soul was there to disturb the birds. There was plenty of fish in the waters, and the birds were snapping up some of the panfish they found near the gently sloped shoreline.

There were already several gulls fishing and floating

at a southern peninsula of the reservoir. The land curved around into a hook, and the birds were gathered inside. Several more birds flew in and joined them. Many of these were the birds that began the flight from San Clemente, others were newer birds that either remained local to the reservoir or had flown in from other areas.

Even though the land looked flat, they were actually at an elevation of more than 4,000 feet at this point. Once they got to Mono Lake, they would be at almost 6,400 feet above sea level. They had been steadily climbing ever since they passed Bakersfield. The increasing elevation along with all their food consumption made them slower and sluggish as they flew.

As they filled their bellies with fish to stem their cravings, they floated in the water that kept them buoyant and feeling weightless. They were now only about 150 miles from their final destination. Within a couple days they would see the shoreline of Mono Lake and their roost at Negit Island.

ᵏ ᵏᵗᵏ ᵏ ᵏᵗᵏ ᵏ ᵏᵗᵏ ᵏ ᵏᵗ ᵏ ᵏᵗᵏ ᵏ ᵏᵗᵏ ᵏ ᵏᵗᵏ

The word had gone out to every laboratory and drug manufacturing facility that they had to begin immediate production on the new SARV vaccine. Synergistic Pharmaceutical was under the impossible task of providing the viral cells needed and instructions for its creation to almost one hundred separate locations. They had a list from the most significant producers to the smallest waiting impatiently for the vaccine. The list was then further split into the closest locales to the farthest.

Cornell was number five when the two lists were put together. UCSD had been made aware of the new vaccine and placed on the first list, although, they were too far away to get the vaccine immediately. They would have to wait a couple days before they could hope to get the new airborne version, although they were still developing the revised injectable vaccine.

Once a company received the vaccine, they had less than 48 hours to get as much as they could make to Travis Air Force Base in Northern California. They were to keep manufacturing the vaccine and sending shipments to Travis until they were told to stop. They were advised that order would not come for quite some time.

Pharmaceutical companies were used to working under tight deadlines, but this was so beyond the call that they began setting up manufacturing branches to act as relay stations to facilitate the demands made upon them. There was not a minute to lose in the race to get the vaccine to Travis in time.

Lt. Col. Mark Washburn was looking over an aerial map of Mono Lake. He had been briefed on where the birds were most likely to congregate and was going over this with his C-130 captains. They were to concentrate their initial efforts over the two islands in the lake. They had to fly high enough not to scare or disperse the birds, but low enough to make sure the birds received a strong enough dosage of the vaccine to prevent them from contracting the disease.

"Not exactly like spraying mosquitoes is it LC?" commented one of the captains.

"No, and God help us all if this gets screwed up. From what I've been told, the ballgame will be lost, and all the players killed off if we do," said Lt. Col. Washburn. "We will probably need to do this in shifts, as I have been informed that we will not get the vaccine all at once. This is why we need to set up primary targets followed by secondary and tertiary areas to be sprayed."

Washburn continued, "We probably won't have a sufficient amount of vaccine to send all of you up. So, Wilson and Haverly, you are the first flight, followed by Evers and Gurley on standby. If we get more of the stuff, I will make adjustments to the first group. But all of you need to be ready to go up."

"Is there a type of bird we need to focus on?" asked Capt. Evers.

"They believe the gulls are the primary target, but as I understand it, this disease crosses all the lines, affects anything with wings, and possibly more animals than that," answered Washburn.

"These big birds of ours are likely to spook some of those birds away from the area," said Capt. Gurley.

"You better make damn certain that doesn't happen," barked Washburn to his pilot. "Again, if we don't inoculate these birds and they fly off, possibly carrying this disease, we won't be able to fly off after them to get another shot. There is no second place in this race."

After some more questions and discussion, the

captains went off to check their planes and make sure their equipment was in perfect working order.

$$\kappa\,\kappa^\kappa\,\kappa\,\kappa\,\kappa^\kappa\,\kappa\,\kappa\,\kappa^\kappa\,\kappa\,\kappa^\kappa\,\kappa\,\kappa\,\kappa^\kappa\,\kappa\,\kappa^\kappa\,\kappa\,\kappa\,\kappa^\kappa$$

Desmond Williams needed to go to the office supply store near his house. It was only about a quarter mile from his door to the front of the store in Irvine. He had always walked the distance as he felt it was good for his health since he sat a lot at his office. He had some unique postcards made up for his company and was anxious to get them.

Williams was a tall and husky African-American that could handle himself easily. He had never had to prove this growing up but knew if he were ever accosted, he would do himself proud. The evening was a lovely 75 degrees with a slight breeze from the ocean. A perfect time to go for a walk.

Williams made it only a block when the first crow hit him hard on the right side of his head. "Shit!" he yelled out loud. He put his hand to the spot and saw blood on it. *Oh, goddamn it,* he thought, *Now I have to get those damn rabies shots.*

He kept going, holding the cut with two fingers waiting for it to clot.

The second strike came from the other direction. This time it was from one of the three remaining Peregrine Falcons. It struck Williams shoulder with its talons and took a chunk from his neck. He wheeled around trying to grab the bird and fling it from his shoulder.

As he attempted this another crow along with a gull

hit him again from the right. The crow tried to stab him in the eye but missed and cut him below it. The gull began pecking at the back of his head. The next moment Williams was covered in birds. Two other residents came out with brooms and anything else they could grab to ward off the attackers.

Instead of chasing off the birds, more came out of the sky and began charging the rescuers, including the other two falcons and a Great Horned Owl. Within minutes, sixty or so birds were attacking the three people, all helplessly trying to fight off their winged foes. Their battle was not going well.

Another neighbor called 911 and reported the attack. By the time the police arrived, Williams was dead and being consumed by the birds. The other two residents were nearly gone as well. The cops pulled out their nightsticks and began beating the birds. The scavengers were either too tired or too full to give much resistance, and those not fatally struck by the police flew off to where they had come.

Five minutes later the ambulances arrived to take the three people to the hospital. Williams was pronounced dead at the scene, and of the other two, both were in extremely critical condition. One of them died on the way to the hospital.

Irvine had its first known fatalities directly related to the birds in the residential villages. It would not be the city's last.

Every manufacturer that could produce a drug was working on developing the newly revised SARV vaccine. Most were formulating the airborne version, but there was still a massive demand for the injectable version, due to all the growing incidents from the birds in Southern California.

The drug companies had every member on their payroll working nonstop and were draining temporary agencies of everybody they could send. The senior management in each company knew this was a fight they could not lose. Drs. Greenwood and Friedman made this perfectly clear and said that the executives and their family would be in as much danger as any of the California residents if they failed to stem this disaster in time.

Manufacturing an anti-virus vaccine is a complicated process. Long after the arduous task of creating the vaccine in the laboratory, the change from producing a viable vaccine in small quantities to manufacturing gallons of a safe vaccine in a production situation is dramatic. Immense and complex laboratory procedures are required to be able to scale such a large production. Most companies are unable to make this transition on a large scale.

Even though each manufacturer was receiving samples of the correct pathogen, recreating it into the vast quantity needed had many complexities. Beginning with the "seed" as they call it, which must be kept completely clean of impurities, other similar viruses, and variations of the same type of virus.

Additionally, the seed must be kept under "ideal"

conditions, usually frozen, preventing the virus from becoming either stronger or weaker than desired. If the strength of the seed varies, it will be unusable as a vaccine.

Upon defrosting and warming the seed, it is placed into a cell factory. This is a machine that causes the cells to multiply. Protein enzymes are added to the cells causing them to reproduce. The growing virus is kept in a container larger than, but similar to the cell factory, and mixed with "beads" which are near microscopic particles the viruses begin attaching themselves. The use of the beads provides the virus with a far greater area, resulting in much higher growth of the microorganism.

After multiple other procedures, the final vaccine is made of a weakened strain of the virus. So not only must the seeds be provided, but the distinct processes and cultures must be shared to recreate the critical steps to make the vaccine successfully. If done correctly, and without any changes to laboratory conditions, the manufacture of the vaccine becomes a matter of how many machines, personnel, and viral seeds they can use to recreate the antivirus.

The largest companies are able to produce a hundred gallons within a matter of hours. To cover the Mono Lake area, an estimated five hundred gallons was needed, and then that would barely cover the entire region and nothing further. To blanket all the targets in San Francisco would take a minimum of twenty-five hundred gallons.

The Mono Lake supply needed to be completed and shipped to Travis Air Force Base within twenty-four hours.

By mid-afternoon, the gulls at the South Haiwee Reservoir were on the wing once more. Filled with fish, they were more sluggish than their usual quick and light flight. Numerous other gulls also flew off with them and were heading in the same direction. Some of the crows also had rejoined the diseased birds, and together they made a contrast of mostly black and white against the dull tan background below them.

The migrating gulls stayed low to the ground for a while. It was harder to fly this way, but they knew they were being hunted and decided not to use the currents above them to bolster their flight. The other gulls went straight for the air currents knowing they could glide more easily at that elevation.

They had gone only a few miles when Snake Pit came up behind them. He approached as quietly as the big Apache would allow him. He was able to come just below the flock of gulls, and when he was under the confused birds, he brought the copter straight up and caught many of the birds in the swirling rotor ripping them to shreds. Blood and feathers splashed all over the helicopter along with body parts that went flying through the air.

Snake Pit took out most of the gulls, and the few remaining birds were flying off in each direction. The pilot aimed the rotors at every bird he could reach and hacked up most of the individual birds before they could get too far out of range.

"Yeah! Take that you bastards!" Preacher yelled with each successful strike. He was pointing out the birds as Snake Pit maneuvered the Apache starboard, then to port. The copter was faster than the gulls. The baffled birds could not react in time or get out of the way of the swirling death machine.

Snake Pit said to his co-pilot, "What about that group down there at seven o'clock?"

Preacher looked below him at the group of birds and answered, "I think they are too low for us, Snake. They are hugging the hard deck. We should keep an eye on them and hit them when they fly higher."

"Roger that," answered Snake Pit. "Did we get all of these mothers?"

"I can't see anymore, but with all the blood and guts around me, my visibility is diminished," replied Preacher.

"The major isn't going to be too pleased with the mess we made," laughed Snake Pit.

"No, but he will like the results. I counted eighteen birds no longer a threat," said Preacher.

"Same," said the pilot. "What if we head back quickly and get our bird cleaned off from the rest of the targets and return back?"

"What if we lose the other group?" asked Preacher.

"We found them this time, and we know where they are now. We could get to the base and be back here in an hour and change. We will find them again, probably only a few miles north of here," said Snake Pit.

"From what little I can see, they don't seem to be

moving quickly, do they? Okay, roger that, let's head back to base. I'll report in and tell them what we got," said Preacher.

The diseased birds flew even lower once the helicopter showed up, and was only about fifty feet above the desert floor. They did not increase their elevation until fifteen minutes after the machine left. They carefully climbed after that, looking around as they did. Occasionally a crow would double back and then rejoin the group moments later. This continued for the next half hour.

Then the birds began to split up as if they sensed another attack coming. Some flew towards the right and some left, always leaving about fifty or sixty yards between them with varying heights and distances. A couple gulls remained closer together almost as bait for the helicopter.

ᴋᵏᵗᴋ ᴋᵏᵗᴋᵗ ᴋᵏᵗᵗᴋ ᴋᵗ ᴋᵏᵗᴋᵗ ᴋᵏᵗᴋ ᴋᵏᵗᴋ

When Snake Pit and Preacher got back to base, they got an earful from Major Tom Christie. He saw the blood all over the helicopter and went into a tirade.

Major Christie yelled at his men like an irate master sergeant, "I specifically told you not, repeat, not to get that damned infected blood on you or your machine. Instead, you two took a bath in that shit! This stuff is toxic. It is dangerous to a level we haven't even figured out, and now I have to put maintenance in hazmat gear to clean up your mess. You may have contaminated this whole damn base. You guys are on the ground until we get this whole mess erased from here. You are confined to quarters until I say so."

"What about the other flock of birds we reported?" protested Snake Pit.

"I will get another crew to search for them with the coordinates Preacher radioed in. They are no longer your concern," the major said and stormed off.

The major sent another crew up as promised. They returned to the last known sight and flew further north. Aside from seeing a few gulls and crows flying off by themselves, they reported no groups of birds together anywhere within fifty miles of the last sighting.

"They must have flown off in another direction, major," said the pilot of the second craft.

"Roger, keep searching for another hour and then return to base," answered the control tower.

Natalie Forrester returned to her office where her husband was waiting. She gave him a smile that he had long missed.

"How'd it go?" Dr. Forrester asked.

"It was fine. Have you been waiting here the whole time?" asked Natalie.

"No, I was at the medical facility, but it was a quick visit. Are you hungry?" asked Dr. Forrester.

"Yeah, I could use a bite to eat. Bill, I wanted...," she said hesitantly, "I'd like to thank you for coming home."

"It's where I belong and should have been, here with you," said her husband softly, "Now let's get some lunch.

I'm starved."

Dr. Forrester could see that the pills had worked and his Nat had returned to her more normal disposition. During lunch, he explained about the side effect with the antivirus and her enlarged amygdala.

Because Natalie was a psychologist, she knew all about how the amygdala and hypothalamus affected emotions and controlled anger and anxiety. She understood this had caused problems with her and had resulted in uncontrolled rage against almost everything in her life.

"That explains why I have been hating my work, including my pottery," said a pensive Natalie.

"Yes, and me as well apparently," replied Dr. Forrester.

"I'm sorry, Bill," she said, "Can anything be done? And why do I feel so calm now?"

"I was able to get some prescriptions that the doctor said would help calm you more towards normal," Dr. Forrester explained.

"I don't remember taking any medicine," puzzled Natalie.

"I had to slip them into your coffee," Dr. Forrester said, "It was the only way to get them in you."

"It's funny," Natalie said shaking her head, "I remember going into the class hating having to be there and came out thoroughly enjoying my students. I guess I now know why. You poor dear, I must have been a terrible burden during this."

"A genuine Jekyll and Hyde, but it is good to have you back," he said.

"Any chance of a cure?" she asked.

"They said they were close, but they have to run more tests to make sure you don't get something else in its place," said Dr. Forrester.

"Hopefully, you won't have to keep slipping pills in my coffee to keep me level. If you start to see me going off, get them in me as quickly as you can. I'll try and be a good girl and take my medicine," she said.

Their lunch arrived, and they settled into their meal. Dr. Forrester was feeling guilty about not getting his wife taken care of sooner. He should have stayed and looked after her in the beginning, instead of running off to Irvine.

He made himself a promise to look after things at home instead of putting his work first all the time. Although, this was a tough proposition, especially if the end of the world was coming and he could help prevent it.

ᴋ ᴋᵗᴋ ᴋᵗᴋ ᴋᵗᴋ ᴋᵗ ᴋᵗᴋ ᴋᵗᴋ ᴋᵗᴋ

When Major Christie reported to Dr. Greenwood, his reaction was anything but pleased. "So you got eighteen gulls, but we don't know if these were the birds we were looking for? Were there any other species with them? Is there anything left of those birds that we could verify they had the disease?"

Dr. Greenwood was getting impatient and guessed the pilots killed a random flock of seagulls and not the infected birds he needed to be stopped.

"They were the only birds that were flying together, it

is possible the other birds separated and flew off somewhere else," replied the major.

"We have been tracking these birds all through California, and they are following a linear pattern. They are not changing their direction, they are not flying off to other locations, they are not separating from the other birds, and they are still a threat. You did not get the birds we need, so you better get anything you got that flies in the air and find our birds before it is too late," ordered Dr. Greenwood.

"How can you be so sure?" asked the major. He was clearly not used to being ordered about like a private in his own force. "And how are we supposed to determine which birds are infected by the disease and which aren't? Or are we just supposed to blast anything with wings?"

"If it is in that area I almost prefer your last suggestion. But you need to find different types of birds flying together. Wherever they have attacked, it has always been several different types of birds working together," answered Dr. Greenwood, "Until you find a flock like that and destroy them, your mission isn't complete. And the more time we spend talking means the less time you are doing your job."

Dr. Greenwood ended the call abruptly.

ᴋ ᴋ⸀ᴋ ᴋ ᴋ⸀ᴋ ᴋ ᴋ⸀ᴋ ᴋ ᴋ ᴋ⸀ᴋ ᴋ ᴋ⸀ᴋ ᴋ ᴋ⸀ᴋ

The gulls were back to flying in a closed but not tight group. They headed into Cartago and were finally making some good time flying higher and faster than they had been before. Once they reached the area where the highway divided again, they knew they were less than two days from Mono Lake.

Although Cartago had food possibilities, and the gulls were still continuously hungry, they kept moving northward as their natural instinct to get to Mono seemed to be taking the reins over their hunger.

A few of the crows and ravens seemed to be looking for a possible food cache and were not as determined to remain with the gulls at this point. While the town contained one of the larger populations along Highway 395, they did not see anything worth investigating further. They rejoined the gulls without stopping. Cartago was left undisturbed by the diseased birds.

To the south, Snake Pit and Preacher were reinstated for duty. They were joined with three other Apache crews and told to "wipe any group of birds from the sky." The major decided not to be too cautious for fear of missing the legitimate targets they sought. The major ordered that four or more birds flying together constituted a "group." Notably, if they included gulls, crows or ravens flying together.

For this mission, each crew was given small arms to use if they could get close enough. Their chain guns were too large and bulky to maneuver against so small a target. Again they were ordered not to get any "remains" on them unless they wanted to be grounded until after this incident was over.

The major looked directly at Snake Pit as he said this to his crews. The crews climbed into their respective cockpits and fired up their helicopters.

The other smaller birds that were abandoned earlier still called for their companions. They had flown with the other birds for well over a hundred miles to gain food from their attacks. By now, several had completely exhausted themselves and fell dead to the ground. The disease had taken its toll, and with the further efforts of seeking the group, their small bodies could no longer cope.

One by one they dropped out of the sky or fell from the sage branches they were on. Only a couple of birds remained, and they were disoriented and had difficulty flying any distance.

The larger birds, like gulls and ravens, were disproportionately stronger and felt healthier. It could have been due in part to the amount of food they were carrying in their system, or it might have been a by-product of the disease. Either way, they knew they could make it to their nesting and feeding grounds at Mono Lake if they had to fly day and night to get there.

The first shipment of the airborne version of the antiviral agent was being loaded onto a C-17 Boeing Globemaster III. It was headed directly to Travis Air Force base and Lt. Col. Washburn's crew. It had only two hundred gallons of the SARV antibiotic, but this was not the only Globemaster receiving the vital liquid.

Several bases around the country were standing by with orders to take off to California the moment they had two hundred gallons or more of the vaccine. Because the Travis base was up to seven hours away from many of these manufacturers, they could not wait until they had the full vaccine amount ready. It would be coming from numerous places around the U.S.

The supply would arrive in two hundred gallon increments. And the shipments would not be coming in nearly fast enough to suit the lieutenant colonel. This meant Washburn would have to send the planes out with the same two hundred or so gallons.

It was hoped that this would be enough of the pathogen to sufficiently blanket the lake and its animals, using several planes as needed. If everything were correctly estimated, including the amount of vaccine that was going to be enroute, they would have enough antibiotic to do the job by the following morning.

What Dr. Greenwood and others didn't know was whether they would get there ahead of the infected birds. He received updated reports from Major Christie, and they weren't good.

They had several crews circling the area, and no groups of birds were reported. Several individual birds were spotted, which flew off as soon as the helicopters came into range. A smattering of crows and ravens, along with gulls were in the area, but not flying together. The pilots reported that this was usual when they flew these locations. The infected group of birds had vanished to places unknown.

Dr. Greenwood knew they were out there. He also

surmised that they were a whole lot smarter than anyone was giving them credit for, and that worried him the most. Could they be purposely flying apart now? Dr. Greenwood wondered to himself. He decided to ask Prof. Revere if this might be the case. He called Revere and posed his concern.

"We definitely saw these birds communicating in San Clemente as you said," answered Prof. Revere. "Upon reflection, it could be entirely possible that they have gotten smarter about eluding capture or danger. Many of these birds have flown together for several hundred miles and might have been attacked before. They may be changing their patterns to avoid detection."

Dr. Greenwood told her about one of the helicopters getting a flock of gulls and asked if she thought that they got the right birds. He said, "I am not remotely convinced that this could be the end of it."

Prof. Revere thought for a moment and said, "I wish I could disagree with you, but I can't in good conscience. That also supports the theory that they're flying further apart. I believe you're right and they are still out there. They are heading directly for their summer grounds. If they have any of their instinctual DNA remaining, it would be pulling them closer to what they have always done in years past."

Dr. Greenwood said, "The biggest problem is, if even one infected bird makes it to Mono Lake before we can, then it could begin the chain reaction that we fear, and it's game over. I have the antivirus in the air already, but not near enough to stop this completely. I am calling every manufacturer and school and things are going slower than expected."

"Isn't that always the way?" asked Prof. Revere.

"A few of the manufacturers had difficulties, and the host virus got contaminated," said Dr. Greenwood, "That means they can't even begin again until they correct their procedure and receive more of the effective virus from Synergistic."

"That doesn't help our cause," said Prof. Revere, "I checked with Cornell and everything is proceeding normally, but they won't be able to produce nearly what some of these other manufacturers can."

"Any we get will add to the total," replied Dr. Greenwood, "So keep at them. Do we need to schedule a pick-up for Cornell?"

"Already done," answered Prof. Revere.

"Well thanks for your help Prof. Revere," Dr. Greenwood said, "I'll keep you posted if I hear anything new."

"Thanks so much," said Prof. Revere and she heard the phone click off.

ᛕᚲᛕ ᛕᚲᛕ ᛕᚲᛕ ᚲᛕ ᛕᚲᛕ ᛕᚲᛕ ᛕᚲᛕ

More reports were coming into local law enforcement and political offices about problems from birds. Some of these were caused by the residents trying to capture birds, and the birds fighting back, whether infected or not. Due to the rewards for captured birds, many people were trying to collect on the bounties and were walking into situations they were not prepared.

This included people trying to net seagulls and other

shorebirds, or climbing trees attempting to grab birds where they nested. The birds took this as an attack of their young and did what they would instinctively do to protect their brood.

No one had come across the flock in Lake Forest, yet. Those birds were mostly on the wing looking for food on their own. Only a few birds remained in the area during the day. Mostly the smaller songbirds and a couple of crows stayed close to the tree and the outcropping nearby.

But there were multitudes of birds that were doing the hunting, rather than being hunted. These birds were aggressively seeking individuals that were out and about. Those were the easier prey. Some people only got cut or scratched, although they still needed to be treated with the rabies vaccine. Some were more severely injured depending on the number of birds that were about at the time.

Word was beginning to spread among city officials that a possible airborne vaccine might be available to stem the increase of the infected, attacking birds. Phones were ringing in the governor's office and the CDC about getting their hands on the aerosol and having it dispersed in their towns.

They were mostly told that the vaccine was still being tested and was not ready for dispensing on a mass scale.

It was easier than telling them the truth, as they had to take care of other locations with their limited supply first.

Chapter Twelve

There was now somewhere around 40,000 California Gulls all ready crowding Negit Island at Mono Lake. The brine shrimp was now in the trillions, and the gulls were getting their fill, as were the rails, coots, swans, geese, and a plethora of other species.

The entire basin was thick with birds flying and floating around the lake.

There were over a million birds all fattening up on the alkali flies and shrimp. The eagles and hawks had their choice of game to feed their new broods, and the chicks were growing rapidly under these ideal conditions.

Even the smaller birds like sparrows, towhees, and finches were in their prime element as they grabbed all the insects within easy reach of their nests. The areas around the streams that fed into Mono were teaming with so many different species of birds, it was tough for the biologists in the field to catalog them all. They were studying the migration patterns and attempting to determine changes in the numbers of breeding birds.

The entire area was so dense with winged creatures it sometimes temporarily blocked out the bright California sun from the scientists. It was also not uncommon to see coyotes loping around the area searching for easy pickings without having to chase the jackrabbits and other quick resident mammals of the basin.

Mono Lake was alive with life.

Surrounded by the Inyo National Forest to the south and Yosemite National Park to the east, this was a dream to those studying the aviary wildlife of Northern California.

Less than two dozen gulls were in route to change all that.

The infected birds were still flying in a swarm but not close together. The helicopters had given up yesterday afternoon and returned to their base.

The gulls driven by instinct were on a direct path and had made it to Fort Independence Indian Reservation the evening before.

The birds were now approximately one hundred miles from Mono Lake. The eastern Sierras were bathed in the golden light from the rising sun, but the majestic scene was lost on the birds. The more important thought was they were almost to their nesting ground.

As they flew over the gas station and casino below them, they hoped to discover an easy meal. They circled once looking at dumpsters in the back of the buildings. These were already being scavenged by a few birds, and the flock decided to continue on their northern path instead.

Travis Air Force base sits just east of Fairfield, California, and directly between San Francisco and

Sacramento. The largest employer in Solano County in California, the air force base contained more than 7,200 active USAF military personnel, 4,250 Air Force Reserve personnel and nearly 4,000 civilians. It had been Travis that sent most of the C-17 Globemasters to their various locations back east to await the vaccine. There were thirteen C-17's assigned to Travis and more than half were dispatched on this assignment.

Two of the giant planes arrived back to their base at Travis yesterday evening at 7:30 and 9:00 in the evening. Their precious cargo was off-loaded and staged near the first C-130H holding at the tarmac. Each Modular Aerial Spray System or MASS in the airplane could cover up to 175,000 acres per day when spraying insecticide. The sprayer disperses the vaccine into tiny atomized droplets small enough to land on an insect's wing.

In this instance, the vaccine would be sprayed in a more substantial dose, so more antivirus covered less ground. Mono Lake was 45,000 acres in total area. The Hercules could make three passes if either of its two 500 gallon steel tanks were fully loaded with the pathogen. For their opening salvo, the C-130 would only have 400 gallons from the two shipments that arrived with the Globemasters.

These 400 gallons would cover a good portion of the entire basin. The pilots were briefed to make sure the islands and the lake were saturated first. By concentrating this target with the vaccine in more substantial amounts, the birds would ingest enough of the antivirus to protect them and stop the spread of SARV to them and their colonies if the infected birds arrived or were already there.

They were hoping more vaccine would arrive while the operation was in the works. As the first plane was spraying their load a second would be on the way. That second plane would cover the surrounding areas of the lake making a large circle around the basin perimeter. A third plane would be sent in if the need presented itself, or if the second plane did not have enough vaccine to complete its assignment.

This, of course, assumed that they were not too late. At worst case, if the birds were exposed, they had only hours to inoculate the birds before the viruses effect was irreversible. Because a birds metabolism was so fast, the virus could spread through their system within this short a time. The vaccine was designed to prevent the infection from taking hold. It had not been proven that it could reverse the effects once it infected the host. This was a risk that could not be afforded.

The moment the SARV vaccine was loaded into the steel tank of the MASS unit it was moved on a pallet into the cargo bay of the C-130 and the crew was given the green light to complete its mission. The captain and co-pilot fired up its four propellers and began taxiing toward the runway. The sun was already midway in the bright and cloudless morning sky.

The plane taxied into position and revved up its four Allison T-56 turboprops. The aircraft began to roll down the runway gaining speed. With its current weight, it would need 1,400 feet of runway to become airborne and lift its roughly 85,000 pounds of men, machine, and cargo.

The nose lifted, followed by the rest of the airplane. It was three hundred feet in the air when it happened. An entire flock of gulls crossed the path of the giant plane. They became entangled in the propellers and knocked out the engines on one side. Captain Devon Wilson called out a mayday announcing the plane was crippled, and he would have to circle back and land immediately.

"Goddammit," yelled Lt. Col. Mark Washburn, "These fucking birds have it in for us! I swear to Christ, they are seeking some kind of revenge. Call out the emergency gear and get that plane back here safely, even if you have to carry it."

"We'll have to pull a Sully," Capt. Wilson said to his co-pilot, "And we have to bring it in safely, or we could destroy our cargo and this entire mission."

The "Sully" refers to the maneuver that was performed after a collision with Canada geese forced airline pilot Chesley "Sully" Sullenberger to make his dramatic emergency landing in the Hudson River. Only this time there was no river, and they needed to somehow return the plane and its cargo safely to the ground and its awaiting hanger.

"We are showing two engines out," said the Capt. Wilson, "Numbers three and four, so it is going to lean heavy to port."

"We are too low to circle around," said Lt. Bob MacAskill, the co-pilot, "We will hit the ground before we make the turn."

"Let's pull it up as best we can and will come in from the north," said the pilot.

"I think we are too heavy, skipper," said MacAskill.

"Rev up one and two to full power and let's give it a shot," replied the captain.

"Full power, aye," responded the lieutenant.

The plane lurched higher struggling under its own weight and lack of power. They finally got the craft up to six hundred feet and began a long, slow turn, banking ever so slightly so as not to put too much strain on the plane which could cause it to flip and crash. After a harrowing fifteen minutes, they could see the emergency vehicles lining the runway and aimed the plane to the center.

They touched down at the start of the runway and cruised all the way to the hanger where they had loaded the equipment. As they shut down the other two engines, they could see Lt. Col. Washburn heading their way.

Washburn was already yelling orders to the ground crew to get that plane unloaded and take it to the next C-130H in the line. He shook Capt. Wilson and Lt. MacAskill's hands and congratulated them on returning themselves and their cargo safely.

"We never saw them coming, sir," said Capt. Wilson. "They just appeared out of nowhere."

"There's a lot of snarge around these two engines," commented MacAskill, looking at the damage to the plane.

"Snarge" is a military slang word for the "snot garbage" of feathers and remains from birds that get caught up in the engines or other parts of the plane after being struck. MacAskill could see there was a good deal of blood and feathers across the engines and wing of the aircraft, indicating numerous birds were hit at the same moment.

And there was nothing wrong with the birds that hit this C-130. They were just in the wrong place at the wrong time. But that fact wasn't doing Lt. Col. Washburn any good at that moment. He only knew he was now down one plane and at least two hours behind schedule, and these were problems he couldn't afford.

As the sun rose in the sky, the infected birds passed Big Pine and were nearly to Bishop. This put them less than sixty nautical miles from Negit Island. Very soon they would be flying over the Inyo National Forest, and just the other side of the forest was Mono Lake. Although they felt they were still being hunted, they were flying together again. It may have been to spur each individual bird further on, as they were so close to their final destination. They were moving as fast as at any time since they first left Mexico.

ᴋ ᴌᵗᴌ ᴋ ᴌᵗᴌ ᴋ ᴌᵗᴌ ᴋ ᴌᵗ ᴋ ᴌᵗᴌ ᴋ ᴌᵗᴌ ᴋ ᴌᵗᴌ

Dr. Bill Forrester's phone rang. When he answered it he heard one of the doctors he knew at the UCSD Medical Center say, "Hey, Bill, would you happen to know a test subject we could try out our new medicine on?"

"It depends," said Dr. Forrester smiling, "What kind of subject are you looking for?"

"How about one that might need to adjust their hypothalamus to help control their levels of emotion and anger, by shrinking their amygdala to realign their prefrontal cortex..."

"Okay!" laughed Forrester, "I am not after my MD. But yes, I may have a perfect specimen for you. I think I can get her over to you this afternoon if she's feeling cooperative."

Natalie Forrester was much better under the influence of the medications she had been taking, but she still had episodes of anger and anxiety. These were not as bad as before, and luckily, Forrester had been there during those periods. He talked her down before she broke, or said too much that he knew she would regret later.

Now there was a possibility that he might get his "old Nat" back to normal. He also got her a new prescription, which was helping with the inflammation and itching around her scar. This further helped temper her mood, as she wasn't continually annoyed by the area on her hand.

He called Natalie and caught her just before her next class. She was still in her more normal frame of mind from the pills she took that morning. She was eager at the prospect of ridding herself of the emotional roller coaster she had been on and told her husband that she would head straight to the Medical Center after her last class around noon.

After Forrester hung up from Natalie, he phoned Professor Revere and asked for an update.

"We are actually kind of winding up here," said Prof. Revere. "Now that they have both an injectable and an aerosol version of the vaccine, we are pretty much done. But I'm glad you called, as I have a question for you. Bill, would it be all right if I asked Tory to come to New York when we finish up? Believe it or not, I actually had a couple of projects I was in the middle of before this that I could really use her help."

"I don't have a problem with that," replied Forrester. "She was actually free after the migration reports she was working for at the San Diego Zoo ended. Is she ready to go?"

"I began dropping hints a little while back, and I think she has warmed to the idea. But I wanted to check with you before I asked her directly," said Revere.

"Thank you for the courtesy, Ellen. Tell Tory I will call her later. I will miss her and hope she will come back for a visit," added Dr. Forrester.

They said their goodbyes and hung up.

Dr. Forrester supposed he should check in with Dr. Greenwood or Dr. Friedman, but the appeal of returning to his normal life was too strong a pull. He worried he could possibly be requested to return to Irvine, or other potential places still having bird issues. Bill Forrester was done with attacking birds, and the SARV in general, and wanted no more of it.

He placed his phone back into his pant's pocket and decided instead to join his wife at the university.

ㅈ ㅈᵗㅈ ㅈ ㅈᵗㅈ ㅈ ㅈᵗㅈ ㅈᵗ ㅈ ㅈᵗㅈ ㅈ ㅈᵗㅈ ㅈ ㅈᵗㅈ

Four Apache helicopters also took off from China Lake that morning. Snake Pit and Preacher were ordered to head further north than they covered the day before. Their orders were to go all the way to Mono Lake if necessary to find the birds they were looking for and cease their progress. They were to comb the skies from

Bishop north.

The other crews were told to carefully cover the areas south in circles surrounding Bishop south to Big Pine, Big Pine south to Independence, and Independence down to Lone Pine. Again they were told anything more than four birds flying together constituted a threat and were to be removed from the air.

Major Christie had told his crews that this was probably the last opportunity they would have to remove this threat. He said he was advised from "those on high" that they were out of time and failure to find the birds today would be a failure of the mission as a whole. Major Christie said he was not going to allow that black mark against him, so they had better find those damn birds, or there would be hell to pay.

His voice was ringing in the ears of each crew member.

ᛕ ᛕᛏᛕ ᛕᛕᛏᛕ ᛕᛕᛏᛕ ᛕᛏ ᛕᛕᛏᛕ ᛕᛕᛏᛕ ᛕᛕᛏᛕ

It took more than two and one-half hours to get the vaccine off-loaded from the first C-130 and onto the next. Capt. Ron Haverly and his co-pilot Capt. Lucy Dorsey entered their "Herk" as pilots and crew called them, up the airstair and through the jettisonable crew door on the forward left side of the fuselage.

They could have gone up the cargo bay, but their crew was still making adjustments and hooking up pipes to the tanks and wires to the control room in the back of the plane. Technical Sergeant Jim Simmons would be running the controls at his command board just in front of the MASS unit.

The spray units projecting from the sides of the aircraft were being checked and rechecked by Simmons with everything in perfect working order.

Haverly and Dorsey ran through their flight list. They began to fire up their engines and checked once again with Simmons for his all clear. This time, Lt. Col. Washburn used a Bell AH-1Z Viper, a twin-engine attack helicopter based on the AH-1W SuperCobra, to flush out any possible birds near the runway and make as much noise as possible to scare off any potential intruders.

There were no mishaps, and the huge plane lifted effortlessly from the runway and headed east-southeast toward Mono Lake. It was now after 1 p.m. It was hoped that the first spraying would have been accomplished by this time. Even if all went well, it would take another hour to get into position to begin the operation.

While the C-130 was redistributing the vaccine, another Globemaster III had arrived with another two hundred gallons of the vaccine. This plane would off-load its cargo to the third C-130H Hercules commanded by Capt. Pete Evers. A third ground crew had begun working on this third plane. Evers estimated that their aircraft most likely wouldn't get into the air until after 3 p.m.

ĸ ᴋ⁺ᴋ ᴋ ᴋ⁺ᴋ ᴋ ᴋ⁺ᴋ ᴋ ᴋ⁺ ᴋ ᴋ⁺ᴋ ᴋ ᴋ⁺ᴋ ᴋ ᴋ⁺ᴋ

To drive from Bishop to Mono Lake takes about an hour and a half to cover the roughly seventy-mile stretch. While birds cannot fly as fast as a car can drive, they can fly in a straight line. Doing so cuts a great many miles off the trip. So what birds lack in speed, they can make up somewhat in a direct flight. Going up mountainous areas slows a car also, where a bird can fly at a constant speed if it's healthy.

There was nothing healthy about the birds that had just flown past Bishop. But they were also determined and were now flying east of Highway 395. They were directly over the Inyo National Forest and cruising over the Owens River. Over one more set of hills, and then it would be a straight shot to Mono Lake.

Unlike Highway 395, the birds would arrive on the eastern side of the lake and closer to the island they sought. Negit Island was about ten miles on the northern side, once they reached the lake shore. They were probably less than an hour and a half from the island. It was nearing 1:15 in the afternoon.

Snake Pit and Preacher were still circling around Bishop. They hadn't seen any birds for the last hour, except a couple songbirds close to the ground. They were moving up the highway, and there wasn't much moving there, either.

They continued up to Crowley Lake and flew along the one side. There they spotted several gulls floating in the water.

"What do you think?" asked Snake Pit to his gunner.

"I don't know Snake, I am not to keen on shooting up birds just because they are hanging together on a lake.

We'd have to shoot 'em at every lake in the country," answered Preacher.

"Orders are orders," responded Snake Pit, "If we mess this up we could be blamed for ending life on this planet as we know it."

Preacher thought for a moment more and said, "Chain gun or small arms?"

"There's not even a dozen birds, let's use the chain gun and save the small arms if any get away," answered his captain.

"I'll use the joystick and the MAWS (Modular Advanced Weapon System)," said the gunner.

"Just don't miss," said Snake Pit, "I don't wanna have to chase these things all over the place."

"Roger that," answered Preacher.

Snake Pit moved the helicopter as close to the birds as he dared. Several of the birds below were already beginning to flap their wings at the approaching machine as if to beat a hasty retreat. Preacher lined up his sights and took a deep breath.

He opened fire, and the water sprayed straight up and around where the birds were floating a moment before. At first, Preacher didn't think he struck anything. When the water finally subsided, he saw several birds floating lifeless on the top.

There were still a few birds that seemed confused by what had taken place. Preacher moved the stick slightly and released another round of shots. One bird came up out of the water and Preacher pulled up on the joystick. A moment later that bird fell back into the lake. He ceased firing and looked again when the water settled.

Preacher radioed in that eleven gulls were eliminated at Crowley Lake. They were continuing their search for any other groups.

The C-130 had just come over Excelsior Mountain and could see Lundy Lake in Yosemite National Park. A few miles beyond that they saw the large body of water that was Mono Lake. They banked the big plane a little south to aim for the islands that sat close together at the northern part of the lake.

The Herk lowered its elevation to 900 feet. Haverly and Dorsey came a little north of the lake and slowed the engines to 140 knots. As they crossed the lake, they could see the birds all around the island and in the lake feeding. Despite its massive size, the plane did not seem to disturb the goings on below them.

Hydraulically boosted flight controls provide the Hercules with incredible handling qualities and make the airplane lighter on the controls than many light planes. Capt. Haverly did not need much muscle for his 60-degree-bank steep turn, a standard turn for Herk pilots. Capt. Dorsey told Tech. Sgt. Simmons to be ready. The sergeant stated his affirmative and switched on the controls.

The pilots finished their turn, and when they reached the eastern side of the lake and were past Sulfur Pond Road, they lowered their flaps to fifty percent.

Simmons announced "spraying on" and began shooting his 400 gallons of the vaccine over the lake, birds and anything else the agent touched.

To the south and just east of Mono Mills, the California Gulls that begun their flight from Mexico had finally reached the southern shore of Mono Lake. They could see their island ahead of them and made straight for the welcome sight. They were incredibly hungry and knew that after a brief rest they would do some serious damage to whatever poor creatures they came across.

But for now, they were back to their summer grounds and could nestle in with tens of thousands of other gulls.

The big plane sprayed the pathogen over the nesting birds and gave them a heavy dose of the liquid. As they reached the end of the lake, Capt. Haverly banked the plane again, and Simmons then sprayed Paoha Island with their second pass. They continued spraying while going over the lake as tens of thousands of birds were feeding across the entire surface.

Again with all the squawking and noise, the birds were making, they barely noticed 85,000 pound plane above them. As they were sprinkled with the fluid, they preened and fluffed their wings, ingesting the magic potion. They were now safe from the encroaching birds coming in from the south.

The plane banked once more and made a third pass a little farther south and sprayed the infected birds that were now almost halfway to Negit Island. It would have no effect on them, as they had been carrying the disease far too long for anything to cure them. But it might further help the birds that came into contact with them.

After making a fourth pass, Tech. Sgt. Simmons announced that they were running low on vaccine and a fifth pass would probably not cover too much.

Capt. Dorsey suggested he spray whatever he had left over the shoreline area and they would keep their craft low and level until he was empty. Capt. Haverly agreed and gave the order.

Simmons hit the controls again once they were in position and sprayed the remaining gallons over the shoreline and the vast number of birds on it.

They radioed in their mission status and announced the first wave of vaccine had been distributed.

This resulted in cheers at the base command. The third C-130H was rolling down the tarmac to the runway, ready to cover the rest of Mono Lake Basin. It would take off after the Bell Viper helicopter cleared away any birds from the area.

CHAPTER THIRTEEN

Cheering was going on at the UCI Medical Center, as well. Drs. Greenwood, Rosenberg, Friedman, and Abernathy were high-fiving each other and congratulating everyone around them for getting the job done. Dr. Greenwood wondered if they had been in time. The report of a group of gulls being killed off just before they reached Mono Lake was encouraging but inconclusive.

Whatever will be, will be, thought Dr. Greenwood. He felt reasonably confident in his heart that they had beat the diseased gulls in time. So long as the vaccine did its job, even if the infected birds had arrived just ahead of the planes, the chances of infecting any birds and continuing this pandemic were small.

Dr. Greenwood asked Dr. Rosenberg if she would like to take a ride over to UCI and tell Prof. Revere and the rest the good news.

"Yes, they have worked very hard over there and deserve to share in the celebration," answered Dr. Rosenberg.

On the way over they talked about possibilities and scenarios with the other infected birds all up and down California. This was a short-lived victory, and they still had much to accomplish. But just knowing that the tools were available and that they halted a probable world-threatening situation was enough to concern themselves with today.

As they pulled up to the campus, they were talking about how much longer they might need Prof. Revere and the other scientists so they could advise the team.

"I would give it at least another week," said Dr. Greenwood, "We still don't know how effective the antivirus is, as this was our first real field test."

"Plus we don't have a cure for the original vaccine, and maybe they could assist with that?" said Dr. Rosenberg.

"Well, Pat, they are not medical doctors," commented Dr. Greenwood. "Besides, I got a call from Dr. Mueller at UCSD Medical, and he said they were going to try a new medication out on Forrester's wife that he believed would reverse the effects of the first vaccine."

"Funny how everything seems to go in a circle," said Dr. Rosenberg, "It all began with Forrester, Revere, and that young girl..."

"Tory McKnight," finished Dr. Greenwood.

"Right, and McKnight, and here is the end of it with the same people," she said.

"At least let's hope it is the end of it," commented Dr. Greenwood. "I am ready to move onto something else. I am sick of birds."

"You say the same thing with every threat we have dealt with," laughed Dr. Rosenberg. "We get to the end of something, and you want to run off and work on some new crisis. Don't you ever rest?"

"I can rest when I'm dead," he said, "And if the world ever quits developing a new disaster all the time, perhaps then."

"It seems like every year we get closer and closer to going the way of the dinosaurs," said Dr. Rosenberg. "It just finds new ways to try and speed us there."

"Now remember Pat, today is a celebration, don't bring us down dwelling on such thoughts," chided Dr. Greenwood. "We'll have plenty of time to discuss depressing subjects like that on another day."

Dr. Rosenberg smiled at Dr. Greenwood giving him a mock salute and said, "Yes, sir. You are right. One crisis per day is enough for this old gal."

"Again, we aren't quite done with this one, yet," said Dr. Greenwood, "There are still lots of infected birds spreading this disease. Until we eradicate this virus completely, our job isn't finished."

By now, they had reached Prof. Revere's laboratory, and they entered without knocking. Prof. Revere and Tory were hunched over two separate microscopes and did not hear their guests coming from all the noise of the birds in the room.

Dr. Greenwood tapped Prof. Revere's shoulder, and she startled. He apologized to Prof. Revere, and the activity next to her and the sound of voices made Tory jump as well.

"What a grand entrance I make," laughed Dr. Greenwood.

"Sorry, but we weren't expecting company today," Prof. Revere spoke loudly over the birds.

"Well, I think you will be glad we came," he said trying to talk over the din.

"We just in came to tell you that the entire Mono Lake Basin has been inoculated."

"That's wonderful news," replied Prof. Revere. "Did we get there in time?"

"We believe we did. Although we can't be positive the infected birds weren't there, but we think we got to them before the virus would take hold," Dr. Rosenberg answered.

"That's great!" said Tory. "Does this mean I get to go to New York now?"

"Well, maybe not quite yet," said Dr. Greenwood. "We still have some wrapping up to do, and we don't know how well this will work in the field yet, so there is some testing that needs to be done."

"Oh great," said Tory, "Now we will get to have more birds in here."

On that note, Prof. Revere suggested they move to her quieter office, and they followed her out of the lab.

Ben Floros was 82 years old and in good health. He attributed his spry condition to his daily constitutionals. He suffered from breathing problems occasionally but was determined to make it to 90 before he gave up. He lived in Lake Forest in a small, but comfortable house.

He left his home at 4 that afternoon as was normal and began his walk. It was a beautiful afternoon as were most of them in Southern California, and he felt good today. As he walked, he noticed all the vultures circling above him.

Not an unusual sight as he knew they often did that. But what was strange is that it looked like there were seagulls and a hawk circling with the vultures. Ben had heard the warnings on the news but had attributed much of the hysteria to news sensationalism. The news stations always blew everything out of proportion. He continued walking and paid no more attention to the circling birds.

Ben was halfway through his walk and was strolling past an open field. It was the hawk he saw that got him first. The talons grabbed him on his left shoulder. Ben screamed in pain, which seemed to bring the other birds down upon him. As he fell onto the sidewalk, he slammed his head and was knocked unconscious.

This was the only mercy he received.

In Huntington Beach, Steve Knoss had a fight with his girlfriend and was livid over the things she said to him. They had been dating for six months, and things had been going well up to the last week. He stormed out of her house and decided to go to his favorite place when things weren't going well, or when he was worried about things. He parked in the parking garage and walked out to the Huntington Beach Pier.

There was no one at all on the pier and Steve was surprised to have the place all to himself. Steve was mulling the things his girlfriend said to him and was continuing the argument in his head the whole time. He was about midway down the pier when the first gull hit him on the top of his head. He yelled to the bird, and as he looked up, he couldn't believe what he saw.

About thirty or forty birds were flying just a little above him. They began screeching and dive bombing Steve. He turned around and started running back toward the beach as fast as he could. The birds continued their assault, and Steve found himself covered in birds soon after. He was fighting them off as best he could, and was leaning against the rail of the pier. He lost his balance and his battle when the birds overtook him, and he fell over the side into the ocean below with the gulls in hot pursuit.

Paula Grainger was well aware of the bird threat in Irvine. She had been following events and had heard about the attacks to pets and people occurring all over California. She had been careful not to be out alone for very long. She had run most of her errands around San Juan Capistrano and San Clemente, where the bird situation was less threatening.

She had run out of milk and decided she would do a quick dash to the local market to get more. She couldn't drink her coffee without milk or cream in it, and she needed it for her cereal the next morning. As she pulled into the market, she saw she had her choice of parking spaces towards the front. She pulled into the spot and failed to notice the people waving inside the store window.

They were trying to wave her off as a swarm of crows, and other birds were floating above them and had already attacked a couple of the shoppers that now lay in the store bleeding from their injuries. They had been helped by the store employees to gain shelter after they were accosted outside walking to or from their cars.

The birds had since increased to a number too large to chance going back outside. The market had called the Irvine police, and the dispatcher said that they would get there as soon as they could. The police department was already too thinly dispersed with all the calls they were receiving about bird incidents.

Paula stepped out of the car and had barely gotten past her vehicle when the attack came. Birds hit her from head to foot and began pecking immediately. It happened so fast she didn't even see it coming. She swatted futilely at the creatures, but there were far too many for her to fend them off. A couple of employees charged out of the store to try to help Paula, but they were struck by other birds the moment they came through the door. This time the birds were not going to let anyone keep them from feeding.

The other people in the store watched in horror as Paula went down and the birds tore at her in their frenzied assault.

All up and down California from Bakersfield to Laguna Beach, birds were tormenting and murdering residents. And the longer it went on, the greater the number of birds that became involved.

The bird population was anything but static. This meant that other birds were moving throughout the state, up and down the coast. The birds were as fluid as the ocean beneath them. They traveled over vast territories, and they were beginning to cover a great deal of ground. Not as much as the migrating birds, but they often moved from one town to the next.

People continued filling up medical centers after being injured by the winged assailants. The CDC would broadcast warnings without interruption on every television and radio station, along with local newspapers, about how imperative it was to seek immediate medical attention if injured by a bird.

$$\kappa \ \kappa^\kappa \kappa \ \ \kappa \kappa^\kappa \kappa \ \kappa \kappa^\kappa \kappa \ \kappa^\kappa \ \ \kappa \kappa^\kappa \kappa \ \kappa \kappa^\kappa \kappa \ \ \kappa \kappa^\kappa \kappa$$

A bigger concern was the demand for the antivirus was gravely outpacing the supply. This was magnified by the need of aerosol vaccine that was being produced in more significant numbers. It was a genuine catch-22 to treat the disease or treat the injuries. There wasn't enough personnel and materials to do both.

The potential carriers were growing in number. As known by Dr. Greenwood and the ornithologists, the birds were congregating with each other adding to their numbers with each passing day. Whatever the species, they had an allure to the infected birds. Once they had the disease and tasted flesh, they increased the overall threat.

There still remained the potential for the SARV to spread far and wide if these birds continued to flourish. Eventually, the diseased birds would infect other migratory birds heading to new places in North America and beyond.

These were arguments that Dr. Rosenberg knew well. She couldn't help thinking about how bad this could all get if not wholly curtailed. She knew Henry Greenwood also knew it.

They were crowded into Prof. Revere's small makeshift office. Dr. Greenwood was telling the two women about where things stood at that moment. Dr. Rosenberg respected the doctor deeply. She had seen him under tremendous pressure like this before.

Regardless of the tremendous authority Dr. Greenwood carried, he never acted "above it all" or misused his power. She knew she also shouldered a great deal of weight in the federal government. But Dr. Greenwood's influence and control were far more significant than hers. He always treated her as an equal, in spite of it.

One of his favorite expressions was that you "Could get more flies from a tablespoon of honey than a gallon of vinegar." She knew it, as Dr. Greenwood had worked this theory on her many times before.

But the doctor could be adamant when the need called for it. He was empathetic to a point, after that he demanded results, no matter the circumstances. She had seen him ping-pong back and forth within minutes, depending on whom he was dealing with at the moment, from a gentle, soft-spoken soul to a tyrant refusing any excuses. He always seemed to grow six inches before one's eyes when he was the latter.

Dr. Rosenberg was watching him be his most charming self with Prof. Revere and McKnight. All the while, he was coaxing more work and results from them. She smiled inside but did not dare show it on her face.

ᵏ ᵏᵗᵏ ᵏ ᵏᵗᵏ ᵏ ᵏᵗᵏ ᵏ ᵏᵗ ᵏ ᵏᵗᵏ ᵏ ᵏᵗᵏ ᵏ ᵏᵗᵏ

Lt. Col. Washburn was getting his next orders from his government. The next areas that were to be sprayed were certain targeted areas of San Francisco, most notably around the landfills and salt marshes. There

were many of these, and the total of the spraying area
would require a great many planes heading in several
directions around the city.

Add to that he was down one C-130H from the bird
collision off the runway. With only three of the four
total specialized aircraft using the MASS system, this
would be a nonstop, almost touch-and-go operation. He
was ordered to get them into the air the moment he
received enough vaccine to fill the tanks.

Lt. Col. Washburn knew there were two more C-130s
in Youngstown, Ohio, that were partially modified for
spray operations, but these temporary spares would only
be used in a dire emergency. He would need to lose
another aircraft before he would consider pulling either
of those in. Primarily because it would take longer to
prepare them for service than he could spare.

The ground crews were working furiously to repair
the damage done to the fourth airplane. The birds had
done a pretty thorough job on the two engines. Lt. Col.
Washburn was told it would be at least another day
before it was operational and ready for flight.

At his rate, thought Lt. Col. Washburn, *we will be
doing this for the next month.* Washburn's only hope was
that he was averting the crisis he was told about by Dr.
Greenwood.

The first C-17 Globemasters at Travis had left early
that morning to head back east to retrieve more vaccine.
Planes were crisscrossing the continent to keep the base
supplied with the all-important fluid.

As they were leaving the UCI campus where they had visited with Prof. Revere and Tory McKnight, Dr. Greenwood got a call on his mobile phone.

"Good afternoon, Gov. Newcomb," said Dr. Greenwood as pleasantly as he could.

"I understand you have successfully contained the spread of this wretched disease, is that right?" asked the governor.

"Well, let's just say the first critical step in doing so was accomplished," said Dr. Greenwood guardedly.

"Don't play politics with me Dr. Greenwood, I am a master. Is that a yes or no?" growled Gov. Newcomb.

"Let's call it a qualified yes," said Dr. Greenwood. "We were able to prevent the infected birds from creating a full-scale pandemic, but there are a tremendous number of birds that need to be vaccinated before I can say that the disease is contained. This was just the first step in the procedure."

"That's what I want to discuss," said Gov. Newcomb, "We have to do something about these other cities. They are losing the public to these goddamn birds all up and down the state. I am sick and tired of trying to field phone calls, especially when all I can promise them is that 'we are working on it.'"

"I understand governor, and we are doing everything we can to make sure it is taken care of as quickly as possible," replied Dr. Greenwood.

"Damn it, quit sounding like my office," barked the official, "When? Exactly when can I tell them we will be getting rid of these offending birds from their towns?"

"Um, governor, I don't know about 'getting rid' of the birds, but we should begin spraying the birds to cease the spread of the disease within a couple days," Dr. Greenwood explained, "After that, the other birds will die off as they did in San Clemente when the virus has run its course."

"What the hell does that mean?" Gov. Newcomb yelled into the phone. "What is 'run its course?' A day? A week? Longer? These damn things are killing our residents, and my office is getting blamed."

"It took roughly three weeks for the birds to succumb to the disease, and there is no way to treat them until it does..." Dr. Greenwood tried to tell the governor.

"THREE WEEKS!" screamed Gov. Newcomb. "I can't tell them three weeks! They'll have my head on a pike. You better give me an alternative plan right now, and it better not involve any weeks to implement it, Dr. Greenwood."

The governor had practically spit Dr. Greenwood's name into the phone.

Dr. Greenwood paused for a moment. Dr. Rosenberg watched him roll his eyes and take a deep breath.

"There is the chance to see where the birds are gathering and net them as we did at the Bowerman landfill sight. The military set a trap and caught hundreds of them during that. It took a big bite out of the attacking birds there, no pun intended," said Dr. Greenwood.

Dr. Greenwood continued suggesting the governor have his office contact the military commander in charge of the operation, and figure out where and how best to repeat it for the other areas being harassed by the birds.

"I could assist you with that, but I do not know California all that well," lied Dr. Greenwood. "I am sure that you have a good many representatives in Sacramento from all over the state that could help with this."

"Half of them are calling me every damn minute," stated the governor. "I'll take your suggestion under advisement. In the meantime, get these damn birds sprayed so I look like I am doing at least something for my state." The phone clicked off.

Dr. Greenwood knew by the change in the governor's voice that he liked his idea, but wasn't going to say anything of the sort to him.

"Problems?" asked a concerned Dr. Rosenberg. She had heard the governor's loud voice from a distance.

"I don't think there is now," commented Dr. Greenwood, "I believe Gov. Newcomb needed a solution, and I gave him one. Now if he is smart enough to act on it is another matter."

They got in the car and headed back to the medical center.

$$\kappa \kappa^{\dagger} \kappa \quad \kappa \kappa^{\dagger} \kappa \quad \kappa \kappa^{\dagger} \kappa \quad \kappa \kappa^{\dagger} \kappa \quad \kappa \kappa^{\dagger} \kappa \quad \kappa \kappa^{\dagger} \kappa \quad \kappa \kappa^{\dagger} \kappa$$

Dr. and Mrs. Forrester arrived at the medical center near the UCSD campus. Dr. Forrester picked up his wife at her office and said they'd get her car later. On the way over, Dr. Forrester thought Natalie was edgy at best. He was sure her medication was wearing off, and he had to coax her to get her into the building.

Dr. John Mueller met them when they came in. He had worked with Dr. Forrester a few years back on a project and had stayed in touch since then. Dr. Mueller was Dr. Forrester's go-to person when it came to medical questions after the first attacks in San Clemente. Dr. Forrester gave Dr. Mueller a handshake, and the doctor invited them into his office.

The first thing Dr. Mueller did was to order a CT scan for Natalie. She was less than pleased going through the procedure, and the doctor saw firsthand some of her heightened aggression. When he received the results, he showed Natalie and Dr. Forrester the enlarged amygdala on the one side. He explained that the medicine they had developed would return the inflamed portion to normal.

Natalie was apprehensive and was asking the doctor about side-effects and how he knew the drug he'd been working on was safe? Dr. Forrester could literally see his wife changing back into the person he wanted most to avoid.

Dr. Mueller told her that the only part of the brain this medication worked on was the amygdala, and it only shrunk this part and no other. "In fact, we are quite excited about this, as there are many other applications that this potential cure could affect. Think of some of the psychological problems this could help, or even reverse," Mueller was saying.

"Oh, so trying to put us psychologists out of a job, are you?" said Natalie.

Dr. Mueller chuckled and said, "Nonsense, we need you to identify them for us. We are hoping to help them live a more normal life afterward."

There was a single knock on Dr. Mueller's office door, and a nurse came in holding a syringe filled with a yellowish liquid. The nurse handed it to Dr. Mueller and waited. Dr. Mueller approached Natalie, and she stopped him, saying to the doctor and her husband that she changed her mind and did not want to go through this.

"Now Nat," Dr. Forrester tried to calm her, "Wouldn't you like to feel better about your life again? You haven't been happy since we got back from San Clemente. This could return everything to normal."

"It's perfectly safe," added the doctor, "We have been testing this, and the results are amazing."

"Then you can inject yourself," retorted Natalie, "As for me, I think I would like to leave now. Pills are one thing, but injecting unknown fluids in me is quite another."

Dr. Mueller looked at Dr. Forrester and said, "I can't do this without her say so and cooperation."

Dr. Forrester pleaded with Natalie, "Nat, sweetheart, we need you back to your old self. This will help you. Besides, I don't want to see you having to take pills all your life and riding this roller coaster of crazy emotions. That can't be healthy for either you or our relationship."

Natalie paused and looked at her husband's pleading eyes. She had a brief moment when she returned more to herself and said, "Do it quickly, my inner demons are fighting me on this."

Dr. Mueller plunged the needle and injected the medication into Natalie before she finished her statement.

Another C-17 Globemaster III arrived at Travis Air Force Base with 300 gallons of vaccine from three different manufacturers. It was directed to the hanger at the far end of the runway. The antivirus was offloaded and placed into the steel tanks of the MASS unit.

Two C-130s were already in the air and spraying different areas of San Francisco. This load would be placed in the last remaining working Herk and sent to a third location. The flight crew was going over their targets and mapping out their route.

After the initial mishap with the first aircraft, everything that followed had gone according to plan. Now Lt. Col. Washburn was being given new orders to begin spraying both San Francisco and Southern California, especially in the surrounding areas of the South Coast and Irvine neighborhoods.

Lt. Col. Washburn would have to split his team up with one staying at Travis covering Northern California and the second moving down to the Los Angeles Air Force Base in El Segundo. Not nearly as large as Travis, the Los Angeles AFB still maintained a good size population. There are approximately 870 active duty officers, 500 plus active duty enlisted personnel, 1,600 family members, 11,000 Air Force retirees, and 1,500 Air Force civilians.

He would place his second in command, Major Bruce Palmer, in charge of the operation at Los Angeles. Maj.

Palmer had practically grown up in the 757th AS division. He was one of the first lieutenants joining the program at its inception back in the 1990s. The Major knew more about the inner workings of the C-130s and their MASS units than the Lt. Col. did, and in a situation like this was a great asset to the program. The fourth C-130 would be back in service that afternoon and would be sent with another Herk down to L.A. once it returned from its mission and refueled.

Diverting the C-17 Globemasters was another issue. Lt. Col. Washburn and Maj. Palmer was looking at where the planes were awaiting their shipments. Three of the aircraft were in the northeast, two were at the Seymour Johnson Air Force Base at Goldsboro, North Carolina, and another at Selfridge Air National Guard Base in Mt. Clemens, Michigan.

So far, almost all of the vaccine had come out of the northeast. The other planes were still waiting for their prescribed two hundred gallons before they could leave. One of the aircraft at Seymour Johnson AFB had one-hundred-fifty gallons, and it was reported that another hundred gallons were in route to that airfield.

When that plane was loaded, they would change its orders to fly to the L.A. base instead of Travis. Maj. Palmer and his crews would be getting set up there by the time the Globemaster arrived. Lt. Col. Washburn knew they would be working from these locations for a time. He had heard from the governor's office that the problems with the birds were increasing all around the state.

Once again, Lt. Col. Washburn's thoughts turned to

the two spare planes sitting in Ohio. If the amount of
vaccine started to increase he would have to put these
planes into service. He decided to give the order to begin
preparing the two C-130s sooner than later. He would
need these planes, regardless of how much preparation
they required to get ready.

Drs. Greenwood and Rosenberg returned to the
medical center. Dr. Greenwood was on the phone the
entire way getting numerous phone calls from diplomats
and congressional members inquiring about what he was
doing about the "bird problem" and what progress was
being made.

Dr. Greenwood was the epitome of patience as he
repeated the information over and over to each caller. Dr.
Rosenberg was grateful he was handling these calls, as it
meant she did not have to do it. She had been on the hot
seat many times before, and it was never a comfortable
place to be. Dr. Rosenberg was happy to let Dr.
Greenwood sit there in her place.

Dr. Greenwood called Lt. Col. Washburn and received
an update that seemed to satisfy him. He, in turn, called
Gov. Newcomb and passed the information as he
promised. The governor wasn't friendly during the call
but seemed appeased that some forward motion was
finally being shown. He left Dr. Greenwood with the
threat of his job once more as he ended the conversation.

Dr. Greenwood shook his head and wondered how
that man ever got elected? He already knew the answer,

of course, as politicians always wore two extremely
different faces. One for the public, and the other for
anyone else working with them, or trying to, like Dr.
Greenwood.

k k k k k k k k k k k k k k k k k k k k k

Bodies, or at least what was left of them, were
beginning to fill the local morgues and funeral homes
throughout California once more. The medical centers
were also crowded with new patients coming in injured
by birds.

Police and national guardsmen and women were doing
everything they could to dissuade the birds from
attacking. But short of shooting into the air at every
bird they could see, there was little they could do to
prevent the onslaught.

There were still several random shootings going on,
and seldom, with rare exceptions, did any of the bullets
hit their intended mark. The jails were getting crowded
with vigilantes attempting to take care of the threat on
their own. The judges punished them with hefty fines
and warned the perpetrator that if they appeared before
them again, it would result in serious jail time.

The military and local law enforcement were doing
what they could to trap the birds. The governor did
indeed have his office contact mayors and city officials
and suggested they try catching the birds using bait and
destroy them that way.

Sometimes this worked and several birds were
captured and killed, but just as often the bait went

rancid and smelled up the area where it was placed. If it wasn't put near a section that the birds frequented, then it was all for naught, especially as the birds they were trying to capture were quite proficient at securing food themselves.

Now that the need for birds was no longer a viable market, no one else was trying to catch birds to sell to the labs. So even the help that officials were getting before from residents disappeared.

Some of the smaller birds had died off. The CDC and animal control warned people that if they found a dead bird, they were to cover it as best they could without coming into contact with it. They needed to call the police or animal control to remove the dead animal safely. Naturally, this puts an even greater strain on the sheriffs and police trying to answer the many calls coming in. Boxes of rubber gloves and hazard bags were now a prerequisite in the trunks of many police cars.

Pellet and Bb guns had sold out of local markets, as had CO_2 cartridges. These were not as dangerous and made less noise than pistols and rifles. The police mostly ignored calls that came in about these shooters and secretly hoped the people using these guns were successful in helping rid them of the menace.

Relief could not come soon enough to Southern California.

CHAPTER FOURTEEN

Lt. Col. Washburn had passed on the order to establish the second location at Los Angeles. Major Palmer flew down in one of the two C-130s with the rest of the ground crew assigned to that location.

The first Globemaster from Seymour Johnson AFB was already in the air and heading to that base as well. A second Globemaster was about ready to take off for Travis with another 200 gallons of vaccine for the northern operation. The shipments were still much slower than anyone hoped, but at least they were coming on a more frequent basis.

Lt. Col. Washburn hoped they could get enough to keep both operations going. He was hearing from Dr. Greenwood and the governor's office regularly. He didn't mind Greenwood so much, but the governor's office was an unpleasant interruption in his day. Every now and then Gov. Newcomb would call and begin yelling at the lieutenant colonel about the slow progress he was making.

Reasonableness obviously wasn't something this governor practiced. Dr. Greenwood, on the other hand, promised to apply whatever additional pressure he could to the manufacturers he had working on the vaccines. They had to get more of it made and shipped in a shorter time. Washburn appreciated the grasp Dr. Greenwood had of the situation.

Dr. Greenwood was good to his word, he pleaded with some and threatened others that were in charge of producing the antivirus. He tried to apply the correct motivation to the right companies. Dr. Greenwood asked Dr. Rosenberg to assist as he knew she could use the same tactics he would, plus he was becoming exhausted from endless hours on the phone.

Between the two, they were able to coax thirty percent more vaccine from the companies by the next day. They were hopefully only days to a week away from having all the immediate areas sprayed.

Dr. Friedman was busy crafting public service announcements with television and radio stations and newspapers. She was also coordinating the injectable vaccine with medical centers needing it most. She and Dr. Abernathy had advised most medical offices and urgent care centers where to direct their patients until enough injectable vaccine could fill the pipeline to cover what they needed.

The CDC was in touch with colleges and companies working on this part of the problem. UCSD was producing as much as they could, as were several drug manufacturers in California. They were not yet getting ahead of the curve against the demand for the vaccine.

Because of the speed of the virus overcoming the person's system, the CDC was particularly concerned that some of the people waiting for treatment might not receive the vaccine in time. They had seen this firsthand in San Clemente. Several patients who waited a matter of days became too sick to be cured.

It was suggested that possibly some of the companies

working on the aerosol vaccine should switch to the injectable vaccine, but that was quickly rejected. The best way to stop SARV was to cure the carriers of the disease rather than treat it afterward. They had to prevent the disease from spreading any further among the animal population.

Another case for the aerosol was the virus spreading into mammals like it had done in San Clemente with a coyote and raccoons. How could they know that a mammal had not come into contact with a diseased bird? Whether the bird attacked and injured the mammal, or the bird had died and been eaten, there was a real possibility that other animals may soon be infected.

So far, their luck seemed to be holding. That would probably not be the case much longer if the infected bird population continued to grow.

K K K K K K K K K K K K K K K K K K K K K K

Dr. Greenwood called Prof. Revere once more to discuss the situation in Northern California. Specifically, regarding the chances of wasting precious vaccine that could be used in more critical areas.

"If Mono Lake was the target we were looking for, and if we are sure other infected birds did not veer off toward either San Francisco or the Great Salt Lake, then yes, you could send the vaccine south to here," said Prof. Revere.

"We did not hear of any situations that pointed away from the group we were tracking to Mono Lake, but how the hell can we be sure?" asked Greenwood.

"I understand your frustration, but you can't. We have to look at which areas have the biggest chance to spread the virus worldwide," answered Prof. Revere. "If any of those Western Hemispheric Shorebird Reserve Networks become infected, you would have a pandemic that makes the events down here seem insignificant."

"So your recommendation is to keep spraying those areas just to make damn sure it doesn't spread further?" asked Dr. Greenwood.

"It seems the most prudent thing to do," said the professor, "Plus if we vaccinate those birds, it will eliminate the chance they would become infected later when they begin their migration heading south to this area. Particularly if we haven't vaccinated the birds down here. Is there any chance of getting more vaccine in less time?"

"We are pulling out all the stops to do that, but it is coming slower than we need. We have to keep putting pressure on anyone making the stuff, and we are getting a lot of resistance," replied Dr. Greenwood.

"I hear there is not near enough injectable antivirus, either," commented Prof. Revere.

"No. Not nearly. Dr. Friedman and Dr. Abernathy are pushing on that front and getting the same results. 'We are doing everything we can.' is what they are being told," said Dr. Greenwood. "I am concerned about the further spread down here. Any chance this is affecting other animals or other birds that might be heading south or east from here?"

"I don't think you need to worry about the bird's side of it. This time of year they are all heading north or are already where they want to be. The other animal question has crossed my mind, as well. I really don't have an answer for that," said Prof. Revere.

"Nor do we want to think about it," commented Dr. Greenwood.

"Not really," the professor agreed.

"Well, I have ordered a second operation to begin spraying down here," said Greenwood, "We have to begin containing this problem, and soon," said Dr. Greenwood. "But I won't divert all the aerosol like I was thinking of doing. We will continue to spray up north in the areas we identified. I think you're right professor, we need to be safe rather than sorry." He thanked her and hung up.

$$\text{k} \leftarrow^{\leftarrow} \leftarrow \text{k} \leftarrow^{\leftarrow} \leftarrow \text{k} \leftarrow^{\leftarrow} \leftarrow \text{k} \leftarrow^{\leftarrow} \leftarrow \text{k} \leftarrow^{\leftarrow} \leftarrow \text{k} \leftarrow^{\leftarrow} \leftarrow \text{k} \leftarrow^{\leftarrow} \leftarrow$$

The doctor told Bill and Natalie Forrester it might take a little while for the injection to take effect, and that she should stay on the pills another day. Dr. Mueller didn't believe there would be any interaction, and he said that it may even help Natalie feel more normal than she has of late.

Dr. Forrester noticed that she had already begun to calm down and that she wasn't as edgy as she had been in the doctor's office. She wasn't herself, yet, but her husband hoped she would return to that state, soon.

"Care for some coffee?" Dr. Forrester asked his wife.

"No, I don't think I am in the mood right now. I feel tired and would like to go home and rest," she said.

Dr. Forrester nodded his head and said, "Okay, home it is."

When they got there, he noticed that it was all Natalie could do to get upstairs to their bedroom. She rarely was this tired so early in the day, and he wondered if it was the result of the drug the doctor gave her. He called the med center and asked for Dr. Mueller.

"Yes, the drug would cause drowsiness and may leave her feeling a little off for a while. We have seen this before. I forgot to mention it," said Dr. Mueller, "The best thing is to let her rest and let's see how she feels afterward. Keep me posted on this or any other symptoms you notice. After all, she is an important recipient, but I am sure she will be all right."

Natalie slept for almost four hours straight.

ᚲᚲᚲᚲ ᚲᚲᚲᚲ ᚲᚲᚲᚲ ᚲᚲᚲᚲ ᚲᚲᚲᚲ ᚲᚲᚲᚲ

It was not uncommon anymore to see military trucks containing armed personnel cruising around Southern California. Many towns had called the governor's office requesting assistance for their insufficiently numbered police force to help handle their bird problem.

The sheriff's office brought on volunteers to help go around and retrieve any birds or animals that had been found dead. Even if the animals were roadkill, all their corpses were sent to labs for testing for SARV. They needed to track any infected birds and make sure that mammals weren't becoming infected.

The results on the mammals all returned normal, except one raccoon which showed mammalian rabies. The birds, on the other hand, showed SARV in their systems in all but a few birds. It seemed the disease caused the death of these small birds at a much higher and faster rate than with larger birds.

CHAPTER FIFTEEN

Two days later, C-130's were flying over the Great Salt Lake and throughout Southern California. Warnings about bird injuries were now being broadcast along with explanations on the spray vaccine that was being emitted from the C-130s that were flying over the entire area.

People were told that the spray would not harm them, and might even save their life. The CDC still insisted that anyone injured by a bird needed to seek medical treatment immediately, as the injectable vaccine was more concentrated than the spray.

There still remained a shortage of the injectable version, and it continued to be dispensed to the larger medical centers first. A few of the more prominent urgent care centers were beginning to see the SARV antivirus trickle in, but they only received a handful of doses.

The aerosol version was similarly beginning to come more frequently and in bigger batches. Globemasters were now showing up with three and four hundred gallon batches. Within a few more days, all of Southern California would have received at least one spraying of the antivirus.

The bird assaults continued around the area, and the death toll attributed to these attacks continued to climb. In Irvine alone, the total stood at twelve dead and nearly a hundred injured. Throughout the Southland, the total loss of life had already surpassed one hundred.

The eagles in the San Rafael Wilderness comprised five deaths on their own. They had successfully continued their ruse to get people to pull over to inspect the "injured" yearling, and then savagely assailed the person or persons that came out of their vehicle to investigate.

The National Park Service finally identified the birds responsible for the deaths, and for the first time park rangers were given the shoot to kill orders on the three Bald Eagles. As large as these birds were, they were difficult to spot. They had abandoned their nest and were flying around the area covering the nearly 200,000 acres of the wilderness and surrounding areas that included several miles.

Towns were getting better in their efforts to capture offending birds and were placing traps in identified locations where birds were gathering. They had now rid themselves of several hundred birds through their combined efforts.

Some of the cities had volunteers and law enforcement officials cruising around towns and outlying areas searching for clusters of birds that were roosting together. They knew it would be ineffective to shoot the birds, but once officials located the area, they set a trap to catch the birds resulting in more success. Since the birds were continually seeking food, they now knew it would not take long to determine if this would work.

Dr. and Mrs. Forrester returned to the clinic. Natalie had received a second CT scan, and the results were being discussed with Dr. Mueller.

"Quite a bit of difference between the two," said the doctor as he showed them the scans, "This looks normal compared to the first scan. How are you feeling?"

Natalie replied, "I do not have the rages I was having before. I also don't seem to be angry at my job, home, or other situations like driving, like I was earlier."

"What do you think, Bill?" Mueller asked.

"Greatly improved," Dr. Forrester said, "I was very concerned with all the sleeping she was doing yesterday and the day before. But when she was up and about, she was more like the girl I married."

The couple smiled at each other and Dr. Forrester squeezed his wife's hand.

Dr. Mueller said, "We have tried this on a few other people, and they also reported sleeping a lot after the drug was administered. I think it is just the brain trying to reboot itself. But so far the results have been most gratifying. I think we may be on the way to a cure."

"We can't thank you enough for helping Natalie first," commented Dr. Forrester. "We think we can return to our normal lives now."

Natalie also thanked the doctor and promised she would call him immediately if she had anything to add that might help their assessment.

ᴋᴛᴋ ᴋᴛᴋ ᴋᴛᴋ ᴋᴛᴋ ᴋᴛᴋ ᴋᴛᴋ ᴋᴛᴋ

Drs. Greenwood, Friedman, Abernathy, and Rosenberg were all sitting in Dr. Greenwood's office. He was giving the latest debriefing about the situation.

"We have covered two-thirds of the identified trouble spots in Southern California, and all of the three primary WHRSNs in Northern California and Utah," said Dr. Greenwood. "I plan to move the Northern California operation south to help cover the remaining areas."

"How far south are you going?" asked Dr. Friedman.

"All the way to the Mexican border," answered Dr. Greenwood. "We want to make sure this doesn't go the other way and pop up further south."

"I think that's a smart move," agreed Dr. Rosenberg. "The last thing we need is this to rear its ugly head again once we leave."

"How are we coming with the injectable vaccines for this area?" asked Dr. Greenwood.

Dr. Friedman said, "Now that we were able to switch a couple of the smaller manufacturers from the aerosol over to the injectable, we are finally starting to make a dent in the demand."

"We still have a lot to go," stated Dr. Abernathy, "It doesn't help that new injuries are continuing every day, although the severity seems greatly reduced."

"There has been a lot of the birds captured and disposed of," said Dr. Greenwood, "Hopefully the remainder will die off sooner than later."

"According to Prof. Revere, that won't happen for at least another week, maybe longer," said Dr. Abernathy, "She said it took that long in San Clemente for them to finally succumb to the ravages of the virus."

"I have heard about a good many birds dying that tested positive for SARV already. Why so much longer?" asked Dr. Rosenberg.

"Those were smaller birds that had died. They do not survive as long as the gulls, crows, and larger birds, especially the birds of prey. They take a full three weeks from when they first contract the virus. We could be looking at as long as that before the spraying started," said Dr. Friedman.

"At least we won't be seeing any new cases in the future," said Dr. Greenwood, "I think it is time we wrap this up. I need to head back to Washington, D.C., this week, and I wish to leave knowing that this will soon be brought to an end."

The others nodded their head knowing that was the final word from Dr. Henry Greenwood on the subject. As they turned to go, Dr. Greenwood asked Dr. Rosenberg to stay a moment longer. The others excused themselves from the room.

Dr. Rosenberg closed the door when they left and said, "What's up? I have seen that look in your eyes, and it usually means trouble.

"I got a call today from the World Health Organization," said Greenwood, "Apparently there is a faction out there that is reportedly using Ebola hemorrhagic fever from the Congo as a new weapon. There is a significant threat these terrorists plan to begin infecting people in this and other countries. You and I have been asked to be involved in making damn sure this doesn't happen. I am off to Washington tomorrow, and

I'd like you to come with."

"Oh well," said Dr. Rosenberg shaking her head, "Here we go again. Just couldn't wait for another crisis, could you? Of course, I'll come along. Ebola. I knew this would happen sooner or later."

Greenwood said, "Thanks, Pat. As I told you before, if they ever quit coming up with crises, I'll take a break. Sorry, I can't give you one now, as you deserve it. But I can't think of anyone more qualified to help me with this, especially as you wrote that paper concerning the worldwide threats this disease could have."

"I wish I would have been wrong on that," said Dr. Rosenberg, "No problem, I'll go tell Alice. She can wrap up anything we need here."

"Mums the word on this for now," said Dr. Greenwood, "They want this kept quiet, so a panic doesn't ensue. We don't even know how real the threat is yet."

"Understood. Alice knows I am often needed elsewhere and never questions it," said Dr. Rosenberg, "I'll be ready to leave tomorrow morning."

She turned and left the office.

Dr. Henry Greenwood sat there and looked at the closed door. He thought to himself, *Out of the frying pan, and into the fire.*

The End

Bibliography

Much of the information secured for this book was gathered through the WikiMedia Foundation and is provided under the Creative Commons Attribution-ShareAlike License. Some of this information may have been adapted or changed to fit the storyline, and should be considered as such. Wikipedia has become a valued resource for all writers and I encourage contributions to their material and their website whenever possible.

Kluger, Jeffrey, July 25, 2014. "The Sixth Great Extinction Is Underway – and We're to Blame." Time. December 14, 2016.

Morals, Javi A., Ph.D. Physics & Neuroscience, Mar 30, 2018. Princeton University,

Gaines, David, Gathered February, 2019, The Birds of Yosemite and the East Slope, www.MonoLake.org.

Barko, Bob, Master Sargent, 910th Airlift Wing/Public Affairs, September 25, 2017, "Air Force Launches Aerial Spray Mission Against Mosquitoes" retrieved from www.Health.Mil.

Content retrieved from www.CDC.gov Page last reviewed: November 4, 2016, Content source: Centers for Disease Control and Prevention , National Center for Emerging and Zoonotic Infectious Diseases (NCEZID)

Advameg, Inc., content retrieved 2019, http://www.madehow.com/Volume-2/Vaccine.html

Schiff, Barry, January 1, 2017, "Lockheed Martin C-130H Hercules: Getting the job done." AOPA Foundation.

Simmons, Andrew, June 19,2018, "Modular Aerial Spray System [MASS]." retrieved from c130mro.com/2018/06/19/modular-aerial-spray-system

Rhodes, Jeff, August 23, 2011, "C-130 Hercules Aerial Spraying." retrieved from www.codeonemagazine.com

Kramer, Mary Hope, Updated article January 22, 2019, "Learn About Being an Animal Behaviorist." Retrieved from www.thebalancecareers.com

Korte, Gregory, February 6, 2019, "Birds strike airplanes in US more than 40 times per day, cost $1.2 billion per year, FAA data shows." USA Today.

Biography

Joe Moore is a multi-genre, award-winning, international author of what are sixteen published works by the close of 2019. What is surprising is all the genres he writes in. Just this year alone he will have a suspense-thriller novel, a children's book for ages 3-6, and a Christmas book to compliment the long-standing favorite "Night Before Christmas." The last is written in similar A-B-C-B rhyming style, but told entirely from Santa's point-of-view.

Moore has already been successful with his popular Santa Claus Trilogy, his thriller Return of the Birds, his short stories, and he won finalist honors with one of the seven children's books in his Santa's Elf Series, and a young adult novel entitled "The Faces of Krampus."

A highly respected author, Moore also is the marketing arm for the North Pole Press. He, along with his wife, Mary, who is the Publisher and Illustrator of the imprint, serve on the advisory board for Ingram Content Group in La Vergne, TN. They assist Ingram with product evaluations and recommendations for other small publishers like themselves.

Moore primarily does author signings in Tennessee, Virginia, the Carolina's, and will be adding Georgia in 2019. Moore, his events and his works may found at the website, https://thenorthpolepress.com.